I0761978

DO NOT MISS ALAN DALE DICKINSON'S
PREVIOUSLY PUBLISHED CRIME-FICTION MYSTERIES:

Charlie O'Brien, Private Investigator
Kidnap Country

The Money Changer

The City of Brotherly Love

For the Love of Money

Charlie's Private Eye Angels

Orange County (California) Confidential

Baghdad Confidential

A Mystery in Laguna Woods

A Theft in Laguna Woods

A Kidnapping in Laguna Woods

A Shooting in Laguna Woods

In addition, a published short primer on:
How to Write (and publish) a Novel

I Love That Dirty Air, L.A. You're My Town

A CHARLIE O'BRIEN PRIVATE INVESTIGATOR MYSTERY

I Love That Dirty Air, L.A. You're My Town

A CHARLIE O'BRIEN PRIVATE INVESTIGATOR MYSTERY

BY PROFESSOR
ALAN DALE DICKINSON

I Love That Dirty Air, L.A. You're My Town

ISBN: 978-1-7326283-8-0

DICKINSON PUBLISHING COMPANY

PROFESSOR ALAN DALEDICKINSON
Chairman and Chief Executive Officer

Bank of America
Vice President and Business Banking Manager (Retired)
World Corporate Lending Group
P.O. Box 3962, Laguna Hills, CA 9265

DEDICATION

Howard B. Crawford, the hardest working man I know, Jan Smoker, my wonderful editor, the best sergeant in the Orange County Sheriff's Department, *Sergeant, J. J. Hernandez*, and his 'wonderful' wife, Yvette Marie, Sergeant Kevin Lybrand, and Honorable Eric Garcetti, Mayor.

Brett Long, my adopted son, sweet Bailey, Dr. Anne E. Ford, the best doctor in the O.C., dedicated Brea Police Department Captain, David Alan Dickinson, his very successful wife, and wonderful and very talented daughter, Morgan and also the outstanding Brea Chief of Police, John Burks.

Also, Big John (one of my real-life hero's) and his terrific wife, Leann (my perfect adopted daughter), Lindsay and Zach Also, the *State* of *California Attorney General*, Xavier Becerra, his great *Assistant*, Marvin Scott, the good Court of Appeal, and the State of California *Supreme Court*. And, my old friends Thomas and Pamela Rose, Marc Mabile, a very good friend, and Ray and Judy. And, Ron and Peggy Edwards, she's a marvelous editor and a great friend too.

Los Angeles Police Department, Chief, *Michael Moore*, who is dedicated to 'Serve and Protect' everyone in the 'City of the Angels', and also, *Los Angeles County Sheriff's Department*, Sheriff *Alex Villanueva*, who is a completely tireless advocate for all of the citizens of the very large and sprawling Los Angeles county.

Orange County *District* Attorney, Todd Spitzer, and *Deputy* District Attorney, Hope Callahan, OCSD- Sheriff Don Barnes, and OCSD- Undersheriff, Robert 'Bob' Peterson. Also, my good friends Simone' Voltz (a wonderful lady and big mystery fan), Parnaz, Cindy, Maria, and our friend Angie, a very nice lady. And, also, Jorge Gomez, Ricardo Reyes and Dana Johnson, a true professional.

My Sister Jan and John, cat lovers like myself, and sister Lisa and Bob, rescue dog lovers. Both of my sisters are absolutely wonderful women, as well as both being quite intelligent and dedicated to helping others as well as pets and animals.

Also, my great bankers, Jason, Monette, Julia, Jackson, Nolan, Sarah, and Jessica, John and Chris, as well as President Donald J. Trump, Vice President, Mike Pence, and William Barr, A.G.

In addition, to all of the very *dedicated law enforcement deputies*, and police *officers*, in Los Angeles as well as all across the great 'United States of America.'

These extremely brave, and completely fearless, women and men criminal justice and law enforcement individuals' 'risk' their lives every day, every day, to protect woman, children and the needy, and the less fortunate people in our southern California communities, as well as our beloved Nation!

SPECIAL DEDICATION

Lynn, you are my bright morning sun light, and you are also, my silvery- shiny moon and also you are my celestial and heavenly stars. And, because of lovely you, upward I shall fly.

In addition, you are clearly my inspiration for writing my quite large Literary Library, not to even mention, my main reason for living!

Also, to:

Mrs. Yvette Marie Hernandez, one of the bravest and most courageous women that I have ever met in my entire lifetime!

PROLOGUE

I LOVE THAT DIRTY AIR, L.A. YOU'RE MY HOME

Lyrics By Professor Alan Dale Dickinson

I'm wanna tell you a story,
I'm wanna tell you about my home town,
I'm gonna tell you a big fat story, Baby,
Aww, it's all about my home town!

Yeah, down by the river,
Down by the banks of the river L.A,
Aw, that's what's happenin' baby,
That's where you'll find me,
Along with lovers, muggers and thieves,
Aw, but they're all cool people!

Well, I love that dirty air,
Oh, L.A. you're my home,
Oh, you're the number one place!

Lovely women (and I mean they're really lovely),
Have to be in by twelve o'clock (oh, that's a shame),
But I'm wishin' and a hopin', oh,
That just once those doors weren't locked,
I like to save time for my baby to go out on the town!

Well I love that dirty air,
Oh, L.A. you're my home (oh, yeah),

'Cause I love that dirty air,
Oh, L.A. you're my home (oh, yeah)!

Well I love the dirty air (I love it, baby),
I love that dirty air (I love L.A.),
I love that dirty air (oh, yeah, I love L.A.),
(Have you heard about **Charlie** the P. I.?),
I love that dirty air (I'm the man, I'm the man)
I love that dirty air (Owww),
I love that dirty air (a come on, a come on),
I love that dirty air (come on),
I love that dirty air (I'm in love with my L.A.),
I love that dirty air (Aww yeah),
I love that dirty air,
I love that dirty air,
I love that dirty air!

[A different, and brand-new version, written by: Alan Dale Dickinson, Dickinson Publishing Company, Los Angeles, California. October 17, 2019, copyright ©2020].

[Citation: Inspired by, and the original lyrics by, 'The Standells:' Songwriter, Ed Cobb, Universal Music Publishing Group, Los Angeles, California, 1966].

PREFACE

You probably have heard the term ‘dancers', all different types of professional dancers, use it all the time. It goes like this just in case you have never heard it: "I am going to bring it (everything I've got) and I am darn well going to leave it all out on the dance floor, no matter what it takes!" Think ‘American Idol' and ‘Can You Dance', et cetera—TV shows from Hollywood. Those contestants cry, argue, and schmooze with the judges and dance and sing their little hearts out and behinds off. And then they all "*Leave It On the Dance Floor*!"

Private Investigators (PI's) and Detectives, both police detectives as well as private detectives and investigators who are self employed, do pretty much the same thing. The only difference between what Old Charlie sees is that, *sometimes*, just every once-in-awhile, these types of individuals have to leave some of their ‘blood and/or some of their body parts and/or their lives, on the floor (i.e. leave it on the job!)

This applicable quote of unknown origin is sort of like the Private Investigator's own personal mini version of their vocationally *perceived* mission statement.

CHAPTER ONE

SARGE, THAT IS TO SAY, Sargent J. J. Hernandez, is lying in ICU (Intensive Care Unit) in critical condition at the famous and quite old and Historic Landmark, the 'California Memorial Center.' It is located in right downtown L. A. (Los Angeles) at the connection of the llO (Harbor Freeway) and the 10 (San Bernardino Freeway).

This is one of the busiest intersections in all of California and most likely the whole United States of America. From very seriously injured, Sarge's hospital bed, he could see all of the 'hustle and bustle' of Mid-town Los Angeles.

He could also see the crystal clear and dark royal blue Pacific Ocean around *Santa Monica*, as well as from the other window, the lovely snow-capped San Gabriel Mountains. On 'a clear day' he could see most of downtown L. A. and 'La, La Land' (Hollywood), albeit, when *smoggy* (*I love that dirty air, L. A. you're my town*).

He has all kinds of tubes, wires, breathing apparatus, and IV's (intravenous) attached all over his very injured body. Sarge was in excruciating and debilitating pain, however, being the very tough man that he is, he did not cry, even a little, nor did he cry out in suffering like several of the men in the nearby hospital beds in the ICU.

Sarge leaned over the edge of his hospital bed, and said to Charlie, “I hate to say this my all -time favorite, Jefe, but the last time you were in a hospital bed you cried like a baby.”

Charlie shot back, immediately, “No, I did not my son, it was the guy in the next bed that was crying, not old Charlie.” And he quickly added, “I am as tough as nails, and I never cry and when the bad guys see me coming, they always step aside.”

It just so happens that our man Charles ‘Charlie’ Warner Kennedy O’Brien the famous and/or infamous, depending on whom you talk to, L. A. (Los Angeles) internationally known PI, (Private Investigator) was born at that very hospital, however, he will not tell Sarge in what year?

Sarge and Charlie, his favorite all time *Jefe*, were bringing down a L. A. Blood gang member (Red *bandanas*) in the Watts area of Compton. Charlie used to work in that area way back in the day, and Charlie told Sarge that the people of Watts were some of the nicest, quite respectful and most *gracious* people anywhere in the nation.

He still has lots of friend there and goes to weddings, ‘*quinceañeras*’ and parties there, every chance he gets. Charlie does not ‘put away’ as many Coronas as he did when he was a Lieutenant with the LAPD, but he still loves to have a good time.

Charlie told Sarge that while he was Caucasian [white] on the outside, on the inside he was Latino, African American and Asian. Because he grew up in the barrio of La Puente/El Monte in the San Gabriel Valley, he loves Latina women with long dark black hair, and big brown and mysterious looking eyes, with long legs, of course.

Sarge told Charlie when he said that, "Jefe, that sounds like my lovely Yvette." And Charlie quickly agreed, as he had known Yvette for a long time and thinks she is the best. Also, that she deserves a metal for putting up with Sarge for all of these years.

He likes to sing, off key naturally, "I love L. A. (remember that old *Randy Newman* hit song) and I love Compton too." Charlie is a 'want to be' rock n' roll star, he just does not have the voice, the memory, the range, the stage presence, nor the vocal range to pull it off, *sorry Charlie*.

Sarge's wife, *Yvette 'Marie' Murrieta* (she uses her maiden name for work) was sitting calmly, albeit, very concerned and worried at his hospital bedside. She had been sitting in that chair for three days now, without much sleep and very little food. She was worried, very, but did not show it, as she did not want Sarge to worry about her.

Sarge told Charlie that when he first met his lovely and quite charming wife, "It was love at *first sight*." And that, "She was definitely the perfect woman for me. And the best woman that I had ever met." And Charlie could tell that he very sincerely felt that way, no doubt.

His wife was a LT (Lieutenant) with the *'Robbery and Homicide'* unit of the great OCSD (Orange County Sheriff's Department) where Sarge also works. Of late, he has been on loan to Charlie by the good OCSD *Don Barnes, Sheriff* and Chief Coroner.

Word on the 'Streets' was don't mess with LT. *Yvette Murrieta*, or she will put you down! The Santa Ana barrio gang bangers, however, liked and respected her because she had helped several of them to stay out of Lambeau Detention Center in Orange (just off of the Garden Grove -22 Freeway) and/or state prison.

They all knew that she was always 'straight' with them. She never 'hassled' them just to show off like some of the other deputies (the bad apples, so to speak).

Sarge and Yvette have a wonderful and very close family, mostly living in the OC (Orange County) area. Some others were still in Mexico, in beautiful Ensenada, right on the Pacific Ocean.

Charlie just loves Mexico, particularly, Tijuana and *Ensenada*. And he has been going there since he was a teenager [100 years ago]. And he still goes there every chance he gets.

He told Sarge, "When you get well my *niño*, we will all go there together as *Familia* and have a ball. We can rent several 'bungalows' right on the lovely Pacific Ocean for almost nothing. The peso is weak and the Americano Green Backs go a long- ways."

Charlie then added, "And you and I can go deep-sea fishing for Marlin while the ladies can go into town and do some shopping and sightseeing too." Charlie also loves to go shopping while in Mexico.

They have the best hand-made leather and stone articles and he uses them for gifts all year long after he has been down there. He says, "They just don't make things like these in the States anymore, sad to say."

^^^^^

Sarge's quite lovely, LT (Yvette) is a distant relative to the very famous Mexican *Joaquin Murrieta*, Charlie has always been very fascinated with old Juaquin. Charlie wrote a research paper on him just a few years ago. He was like Charlie in a way in that both are either famous and/or infamous depending upon whom you ask!

Yvette asked Charlie, "What happened to my beloved husband, Jefe? Charlie, paused, and then paused some more before he answered her. Then he responded, "Yvette my *niña*, it was all my fault, I am so sorry to tell you."

"I was supposed to 'kick in' the steel reinforced front door, and Sarge jumped in front of me." And he said, "*Jefe* you are too old to go first, follow me old man." And, "Just as soon as he busted the door down, I heard a shotgun blast and then 60 seconds later, I heard another one."

Charlie then told Yvette, "I thought Sarge was dead, but I took out three gangbangers with my M-15 automatic assault rifle in one hand and my trusty 'Dirty Harry' (Clint Eastwood) .357 caliber *Magnum* six shooter revolvers, in my other hand."

"Then, just as fast as I possibly could, only about 30 seconds, I called 911 and asked for a Police emergency dispatch time, and then radioed the Watch Commander at the local L. A. County

Sheriff's Department Sub-station nearby, for back up, as I had not cleared the run-down and rat-infested *stash* house."

When back up arrived, the great LACSD [Los Angeles County Sheriff's Department] brought their armored personnel carrier (APC) with about 20 very well armed deputies, ten were male deputies and 10 were female deputies.

They surrounded the house, and all at the same time, busted into every door and window in the place. They set off several flash-bang grenades as well as some teargas. Then they took control of the situation, indeed.

The back-up deputies, in full armed gear, found four more gangsters and took them out after they failed to surrender. Each deputy carried a M-15 automatic assault rifle, an assault shotgun, and two 9-millimeter automatic *Glock* pistols; one on each hip, plus a K-Bar military knife as well."

Charlie went on talking to Yvette, "If I had gone through the door first, like I should have done, Sarge would not be laying here in immense pain and suffering, it would have been me, and it should have been me."

He continued trying to explain to Yvette, "I am so, so very sorry Yvette, I want you to know, and I think you already do, that Sarge is like a son to me. That is why I call him my *niño*."

Sarge grew up in a barrio just like his fearless boss, Charlie, did. All of his friends and neighbors later in life became either a 'banger' or a cop/deputy. The gangsters in his crib area had a lot of respect for Sarge as, even though he did not *bang* with them, he treated them with 'respect' and helped them do home repairs and yard work as well as assist them with their homework.

Also, another reason that he got along well with the rough crowd was that he was very strong and could bench press 300 plus pounds quite easily. And he also was a Black Belt in Tae Kwon Do and Karate.

They say that Sarge never, ever, started a fight, but he also never, ever backed down from some hoodlum who thought he would make his bones with Sarge. And that poor soul found out very quickly, very, that Sarge knew how to get down and dirty when he had to and was forced to do it.

Sarge always carried a 6" switch blade wherever he went into a high school. He had several very decretive ones and he kept them razor sharp at all times. He never knew what could go down where he lived and went to school.

He bought the knives in Tijuana, Mexico over the years while down south visiting his relatives who lived there and also some in lovely Cancun, on the lovely Gulf of Mexico.

When they were in high school, Charlie forgot the name of the school, Yvette was a cheerleader as well as very athletic. She also was very intelligent, very attractive, and more importantly, much more importantly, she was also very nice.

All of the guys at school wanted to date her just based upon her good looks, but Sarge wanted to be with her because she was beautiful on the inside as well as on the outside.

She had her pick of the litter (sorry Sarge) but she picked Sarge because he was the nicest, most gentle, most caring, as well as the most thoughtful of all of her other suiters. Sarge told Charlie, his BFF, that the day Yvette said, "Yes, I will marry you," was the best day of his life, it really was!

Sarge also told Charlie, that the main reason that Yvette was such a precious and marvelous person, was that she had wonderful parents. They taught her how to be a great wife, a great mother, and also a great OCSD lieutenant.

Charlie could not remember Yvette parents' names, but he really wanted to meet them some day because he had heard so many good things about them from both Yvette as well as Sarge.

Yvette was very seriously ill recently, however, she never complained or asked for sympathy nor pity. She just worried about Sarge, her children, and her parents. And not about herself at all. And she knew that someone in Heaven was watching out for her. Quite a remarkable woman, Charlie felt!

She is fine now and she told Charlie, "My adopted Pappy, I could not wait to get back on 'the job' at the OCSD, and get out amongst the great citizens of Orange County, once again."

When she returned to her office on Flower Street in Santa Ana, California they had a big Welcome Back party for her, which lasted for three days. They had it out on the Patio at the corner of Flower and Santa Ana Avenue.

Then good Captain Jason Danks, Sarge's boss at one time and now his wife's supervisor, invited the whole OCSD officers who were off-duty to come. He also sent out flyers to the local patrol area where Yvette worked, and dozens and dozens of local citizens came as well. Her peeps just loved her; they really did.

Some local attorney, from the Court House across the Street, called 911 to complain about all of the noise. Charlie thought that was funny, and he told Yvette and Sarge, "Just consider the source, attorneys."

The LT said to Charlie, "We have *Fiestas* like that for the *Federales* in Mexico all of the time and they all love it. And we don't like lawyers south of the border either. All they do is talk, threaten, oppress and try to intimidate innocent and elderly citizens."

CHAPTER TWO

THE DAY, AND I MEAN the very same day, that Sarge was discharged from the marvelous California Medical Center in ("I love that dirty air, L.A. you're my town") downtown Los Angeles, he said to Charlie, "Hey old man, thanks a million for sitting up nights and sleeping in a chair in my hospital room with my lovely and very strong, wife Señora *Yvette 'Marie' Murrieta*, prettiest woman I ever laid my eyes on."

Sarge, being the very smooth talker that Charlie's Latino niño is, got the emergency doctor to let him be released four days early. Even though he was still very sore, and still in a lot of pain and suffering.

Then, not letting Charlie say, "Your welcome, Sarge." As he knew that our man Charlie had a very difficult time expressing his emotions and could not find the words to tell his BFF, Sarge, that he was almost scared to death, that Sarge would not make it, and go to his home in *Heaven*.

So, while Charlie was still being so, so very thankful to the man upstairs, that Sarge was still alive and well, Sarge spit out, "*Jefe*, let's get out of this place, and kick in some more doors, what do you think?"

Charlie pondered and did not answer right away, due to the fact that he did not want Sarge to get shot again. While he was thinking Sarge spoke, "However this time Jefe, I will let you go in first, just in case there is another sawed- off shot gun behind the door."

And he went on to add, "Just kidding boss, I would not let a senior citizen, meaning you, go in ahead of me, even if my life depended on it, which as you well know, it might." Then Sarge laughed and then he laughed some more, until his stiches began to come loose.

Finally, Charlie opened his usually continually moving mouth and replied, "Well Junior, you are more than welcome, and I don't sleep much at night anyway. I have a debilitating case of insomnia."

Charlie gets embarrassed any time someone thanks him for doing something that he just considers to be a regular part of his job and that is to 'Serve and Protect' people.

They made Sarge go down to Charlie's new jet black, BMW 750 iL, in a wheel chair even though he fought them 'tooth and nail', saying, "Doc, I feel fine, I can walk," which he stubbornly tried to do, and fell flat on his face.

LT Yvette told the hospital orderly, that she wanted to push Sarge, and he kindly agreed. She works out and is in very good shape, and Sarge always brags about how smart, lovely, kind and strong that his '*Marie*' is. He really does!

Charlie bought his jet-Black Beauty II from **Irvine** BMW, in Irvine, California, just off of the 5 (Santa Ana) Freeway. It is about half way between Los Angeles and San Diego, paralleling the old *Camino Real* (King's Highway) or Pacific Coast Highway.

The General Sales Manager is *Frank Verna,* a real automobile expert and he is truly an automobile professional, he really is! His automobile agency, sells every cool model BMW makes from the inexpensive and yet very well equipped 128i to the BMW limo at about $150,000.

Frank told Charlie, and he was just kidding, "Charlie my amigo, I could put you behind the wheel of a *Silver Cloud* Rolls Royce, for only $350,000.00, you interested?" Then he laughed and so did Charlie, who responded, "Thanks a lot Frank, but only in my dreams."

And *Steve Oh,* the new car Sales Manager, is a great guy and he gave Charlie a really great deal on his fully-loaded Beemer, out the door for only $85,000.00, a real bargain. This is one of the finest road-production vehicles in the World, it truly is. Steve also gave Charlie a very fair trade in for his used, but still in excellent condition, BMW X-3 SUV.

The General Manager of the whole huge and expertly-run automobile center is Roger See. He is Frank and Steve's supervisor, Charlie thinks. He has not had the privilege to meet Mr. See yet, however, he has seen him in and about the very large Irvine BMW automobile facility.

Also, Charlie has not had the honor to meet the owner of the agency, however, he hopes to do that in the near future as he needs to buy a new 330e [this car has a hybrid motor and it gets great mileage] for his lovely Philly Girl, and Steve told him he would give Charlie a great deal on it as usual.

And Black Beauty II, practically drives herself. She has all of the 'bells and whistles', sun roof for the Laguna Beach weather, run flat tires, bullet-proof windows, shot-gun in the trunk, computer black box for GPS and more gadgets than Charlie can even figure out how to use.

Charlie tells everyone he knows that if you are in the market for a BMW (or a *Rolls Royce* or Mini Cooper) call Frank or Steve and they will fix you up in no time, no time at all. All of the staff are just super great people and good friends of Charlie's.

Sarge still had some shotgun pellets in him, as they were not able to get all of them out. They told him that they did get thirty pellets out of his chest and left arm, and they guessed that there were five to ten left floating around in his body.

Sarge never cried, never whimpered, nor even cussed, the whole time he was in the ICU, and then in his hospital room. Charlie told Yvette (Charlie just absolutely adored the LT and he told Sarge that she was the most perfect woman that he had ever met, with the exception of his own Philly Girl, naturally), "that Sargent J. J. Hernandez, was the bravest, most caring, most resourceful, and street smart, law enforcement officer that he had ever met in his entire thirty plus law enforcement career.

He did not add, because he began to get a little bit *choked* up, that he would not 'ride- along' with any other OCSD, or Police officer, he really would not. He knew that Sarge would give his life for his Jefe, and he would do so with a drop of a hat.

Sarge then turned to Charlie, and said, "Senior O'Brien, how about we go get some real grub, that hospital food is for the birds.

I am just dying for some rich tomato enchiladas, refried beans and Mexican rice."

Then he smiled, one of his I want to get into trouble smiles, "I also want a big chocolate milkshake, and some Latino pastries too. He added, "Oh, Jefe, and also let's drive by Mary 'Sees' *candy store*, and get a five- pound box of *chocolates*."

And, "Charlie my buddy, my friend, you cannot tell Yvette about what we had to eat. I am supposed to be on a diet, and she gets upset with me when I do dumb things like this. But a man has to do what a man has to do, right my amigo?"

Charlie's response, "You know that you can trust me, my son, with our little *foodie* secret, no problem, none at all." Then just as soon as Sarge went to the men's room, Charlie hit his speed dial on his cell phone and said, "Yvette *Marie*, your husband is breaking his sworn diet."

"And he just ate all kinds of food that is bad for him, and I tried to stop him for you, but I was just not able to do it." The LT responded, "Thank you for the insight *Pappy*, I will have a nice little chat with our Sergeant when he gets home tonight. Also, please keep an eye out for him so that he does not get shot again, alright Charlie?"

Charlie was always trying to get Sarge in trouble with Yvette, and Sarge was always trying to get Charlie in trouble with his model wife, Lynn. "They just were not able to act like grown men," *Jan Smoker* always says.

Jan Smoker, Charlies ex-CIA (*Central Intelligence Agency*) operative, says that whenever she is around them, she feels like a "referee because of all of their *shenanigans* and mischief that they always get into."

Speaking of Jan, Charlie just called her at her lovely home on the lake in E-town (*Elizabethtown*) Pennsylvania, and asked her if she could fly out to L. A. to assist with some PI work that he and Sarge were working on.

Charlie told Sarge that, "Jan was the best covert operative that he had ever seen. And also, that she was only five-feet-two inches but she could take down perps and criminals that were six-foot-four inches in about 60 seconds or less.

Of course, he also wanted her expertise with covert criminal investigations to help *ferret* out who tried to kill him six months ago when he was on vacation in beautiful Ensenada, with his lovely tall Lynn and Sarge and Yvette.

^^^^^

Jan was the Assistant CIA Director when she retired last year. She was with the 'Agency' for twenty years. And her last assignment was the very *volatile* and *turbulent* Middle East.

Jan told Charlie to tell Sarge "Hello" for her and that she would see him soon, and also that she was very, very pleased that he did not 'bite the burrito' last week. Real glad!

They 'broke bread' at *'El Coche's Fine Mexican Cuisine'* Restaurant, right on Whittier Boulevard in East L. A. (Los Angeles). The food there was out of this world, it really was, and Sarge and Charlie both ate like the little pigs that they are. Sorry Charlie.

Sarge had his favorite meal, a big, real big, chicken burrito, with lots of refried beans and spicy Mexican rice with churrupas and chili-cheese chips with lots of hot salsa. The food smelled as good as it tasted, Charlie said to Sarge.

Charlie noticed this meal, and said to Sarge, "My *compadre*, you are going to be up all night with gas pains. And my adopted daughter, is going to make you sleep on the sofa."

Charlie had a big, really big taco salad with chicken added, a shrimp salad and Mexican pastries for dessert. Then he ordered a fish taco as he was still hungry, our man Charlie as everybody knows, has a very *voracious* appetite.

Neither of them had any of the famous house salty *Margaritas* as they both were 'on the wagon' right now. Back in the day, they both used to 'put-back' a case of Coronas on a regular basis.

Then all of a sudden, who but 'Chuye' from the infamous *'White Fence'* gang from E. L. A., came by the table and said to Sarge, "What's up homie? Long time no see around the barrio, what's happening?"

Chuye added, "Homes, I just saw you with this old, fat white dude, and I decided to just drop in to see what condition, your condition was in, you know what I mean, homes?"

Chuye went to school with Sarge, and he became a well-known *gangsta* in the hood, but Sarge chose to become a Deputy Sheriff. Some said he sold out, but most of the gang-bangers admired him for going 'straight.'

They never 'messed' with Sarge because of that respect and he never, ever 'dissed' (disrespected any of them), and they liked that about him. Plus, Sarge was strong as a *bull* (they called him 'El Toro'). And they did not want to be *stampeded* to death.

Later that day, **Howard Wallace**, Charlies very good friend and fellow Private Detective, called right out of the Blue and said, "Charles my man, I hear that we are getting 'the band' back together?"

He was a distant relative of the famous *'William Wallace,'* the quite famous Scottish freedom fighter two-hundred years ago. Howard took after his relative and he just really loved a good malt liquor as well as a good fight.

He had "heard it through the grapevine" that Charlie was having Jan Smoker fly in from *Philly* to help him and Sarge with some very dangerous criminal investigations. And he asked Charlie if he could come out to sunny southern California as well.

Howard lived in Minnesota now and it was cold, damp, windy, snowy and did I say cold! Well cold and most like cold of Alaska in the wintertime. For some unknown reason, Howard loved the snow and cold, which was funny because he grew up right here in warm and *sunny* Fountain Valley, California.

Howard is the hardest working and most dedicated law enforcement official that Charlie has ever worked with. He used to be the Executive Director of the whole CIA (Central Intelligence Agency) in Langley, Virginia.

Captain *Jason Danks* called Sarge on his *encrypted* satellite cell phone, and said, "My good sergeant J. J. *Hernandez*, I understand that we almost lost you the other day?"

And, then he continued, "I warned you not to hang around with that crazy old coot Charlie, didn't I? Next time he will get you killed." Then he laughed, and laughed some more, he was just kidding, because he and old Charlie were very good friends.

And he added, "On the other hand my brother- in- arms, you might just get old Charlie killed." And then he laughed some more, Captain Danks had a great sense of humor, which is why he and Charlie got along so well.

The Cap used to be a patrol deputy and he was very, very street smart. He also was the Deputy in Charge of the Criminal Detention Center in Orange. His job at the OCSD was protecting all of the good citizens of the OC (Orange County, California).

He also loved a good fight, and if anyone in the OCSD got out of line, and I do mean anybody, even Michael Coors, the well-known and quite infamous former Sheriff and Chief Coroner of Orange County.

Captain Danks was not afraid of anybody, and I do mean anyone. He has gangsters threaten him on a daily basis, as well as crooked politicians, and the most dangerous of all, unethical and despicable lawyers!

Just then another cell phone call, it was from the *boss*, Yvette and she was calling her Sarge, "Honey how are you feeling, my hero? Did you have a real good and healthy lunch with my Pappy?"

Sarge shot a dirty, very dirty look, at Charlie because he knew right away that his so-called friend, had 'ratted' him out. So, he decided to be upfront with his lovely wife, Yvette, and spoke very, very softly.

Finally, after getting his story straight in his head, which by the way, still felt like it was twice its normal size, he said, "Yvette *Marie*, my wonderful and very precious bride, yes I admit that I got a little bit carried away at lunch, but I have a very good reason."

The LT responded, "Yes, I am listening." That made Sarge very, very nervous, so he hesitated for a few moments and then began, "It was all Charlie, your Pappy's fault."

"Charlie made me do it, you know how *persuasive* he can be and he told me, you look very thin and weak Sarge after all of your time in the great California hospital, so you should have a big meal to help yourself recover faster."

Then *Yvette* replied, once again by saying, "Yes, go on dear." Then more from Sarge, "I told Charlie that I should not eat so much because you would not like it, and he made me eat it, all of it. So, you can see it was not my fault, right *my* girl?"

Long silence, very long silence, and then Yvette finally spoke, “Beloved husband of mine, if you keep lying like that, your nose is going to grow like *Pinocchio’s* did. You remember him, don’t you dear?”

Sarge’s response was stone cold silence, Charlie had done it again. Then he said to himself, and *not* to Yvette, “Just wait old man, your time is coming (remember the old saying, payback is a bear) and the big, bad bear is coming for you Charlie my old man, and he is coming real soon.”

CHAPTER THREE

IT WAS JUST ANOTHER TYPICAL fresh and pleasant day in *sunny* Southern (Los Angeles), California. As you all know, it 'Never Rains in Southern California,' even in the winter time, and do you remember that great old song?

It was done by Albert Hammon, a pioneer in the rock industry, and it was written about 1972. It was one of Charlie's favorite all-time tunes, and he met Albert once up at the 'Hollywood Bowl' after one of his fabulous concerts.

Albert told Charlie that he was born on Gibraltar, in the Mediterranean, on May 18, 1944. During the Big One, World War II, his family moved to London, England where he fell in love with music.

He said he felt that he was a much better song writer than a singer, and said that he enjoyed doing that more anyway. Charlie asked him who he had written songs for, and he replied, "Well Charlie, my big fan, I cannot remember them all, there were so many, however, I will tell you just a few."

Then Albert started out by listing just some of them, "The Canadian song-bird, Celine Dion; the Queen of Soul, Aretha Franklin; Angelic voiced, Whitey Houston; the legendary, 'Tina Turner'; The 'Wichita Lineman', Glen Campbell; 'On the Road Again,' Willie Nelson; and Leo Sayer. Oh, and also, the 'incomparable,' Diana Ross! And he thought for a second, and then said to Charlie, "I also wrote for some great rock n' roll bands, like *Chicago*, Air Supply, and The *Starship*, and several others that I forget at this time."

Then Albert told Charlie, "I gotta *bounce* man, you know how it is. But here is one of my new CD's and a T-Shit autographed just for you." Charlie returned the comment and said, "Wow, Albert, I really appreciate it, I truly do."

And, the next time you're in *my town* ('I love that dirty air, L. A. you're my town') Sarge, Yvette and I will take you out on the town for some great Korean BBQ, and go to some of outstanding Venues, and listen to some great rock n' roll and also some good Blues music too, I absolutely love Blues music. Albert, you know the '*Blues Brothers'* were from right here in L. A, right?"

There was very little *smog* today, and that made Charlie happy, very happy, and he was singing his favorite tune, while cruising down the freeway, in the fast-lane of course, 'I love that dirty water, Boston, you're my town.'

Charlie had written a different version of that great song himself, as he had gotten the idea from an old favorite garage band who had written back in the day. Charlie loved old classic *rock n' roll*, Yvette, and Sarge loved it as well.

Charlie and Sarge were 'rolling' back from a domestic call up in *Highland Park*, it is just off of the SR 110 Arroyo Seco Parkway (*Freeway)* that runs between South Pasadena and downtown Los Angeles/ Hollywood. It was the very *first Freeway* built in the United States according to Charlie. That was around 1929 – 1940, the *Depression era*.

Today it is one of the most *treacherous* freeways in the State, as the on and off ramps are extremely short, which makes you 'punch' it to get on the freeway and then to 'slam' on your brakes when you exit it.

It takes you right past the quite famous "*Dodger* Stadium" (in *Chávez ravine*), and also past some very old and stately historic landmark homes and mansions. Some have been restored to their *former glory* and are beautiful to behold, and some are just waiting in- the- wings for that to happen to them as well.

Charlie told Sarge, that "Tommy Lasorda, outstanding Manager of the marvelous L. A. Dodgers baseball team, used to spend 24/7 here at the Stadium, practicing and also playing heated and very competitive ball games.

Then he added, "Tommy lives just across the street from Captain (and also Doctor of Education) David Alan Dickinson of the great Brea Police department, who is also a new member of Charlie's band."

The call that the LASD (Los Angeles Sheriffs' Department) had requested that Charlie and Sarge handle for them (the LCSD were overwhelmed with calls that day due to the big game at the Stadium as well as a protest march right in front of City Hall.

The call they caught for the LCSD was an elderly woman who was sexually harassed by her Tennis Pro and Teacher at her HOA [Home Owner Associations Tennis Facility].

The HOA hired two deplorable low-rent/ambulance chasers to intimidate her to drop her very legitimate complaint (there was lots of evidence as well as many witnesses).

The two attorneys 'Pauly Havnoavic' and 'Squiggly Round,' then hired a PI (Private Investigator) to 'stalk and harass' the poor innocent woman. The PI, an old friend of the attorneys who had oppressed, and intimidated many, many elderly women and men, to drop their honest cases.

The PI's name was Anthony 'the *Pelican'* Pelacono, IV and his grandfather was an infamous PI in and around Hollywood for years. He was hired to intimidate witnesses for trials, young women trying to get work on TV or the movies.

'The *Pelican'* got away with unethical, unprofessional, not to even mention, illegal actions and behavior for years, and years. Finally, the LA District Attorney got him and put him into the men's Central Jail downtown right off of the 10 (*San Bernardino*) Freeway.

Charlie hated old man *Pelacono*, as he said that PI's like him gave his honest and very helpful profession a bad rap (reputation). He had no love for 'The *Pelican* IV' either, none at all.

He said he would love to meet him in a dark alley some time in Hollywood, have a nice friendly chat with him, and then take him to the *Hollywood* LCSD sub-station and have him booked for the same despicable things that his grandfather taught him to do.

Charlie's cell phone rang, and since he was driving, too fast for the old and very dangerous Pasadena Freeway, (by the way, his phone went to his ring tone "Private Eyes" by the fabulous rock 'n' roll duo, *Hall and Oates)*. It was a secure satellite cell phone call from Captain Jason *Danks*.

The Cap had just received a call from the Mayor of the great City of Los Angeles (*Honorable Eric Garcetti*, whose dad **Gil Garcetti** was one of the *finest Mayors* and/or District Attorneys L. A. has ever had) who asked him if he could *loan* Charlie and Sarge to the City of L. A. for a short while to, "a) *Investigate*, b) *infiltrate* and then c) *exterminate* the 'gang- of- thieves' who were causing havoc robbing banks in my town."

Captain Danks told Charlie, when he called him back, (he tries not to talk on his cell when he is driving, unless it is an emergency 911 type of phone call, then he grabs the cell, hits his police type rolling red and blue lights, and floors it. That's the Law in California, talking on cell phones while driving causes almost 1/3 of the accidents on the road they say. Charlie did not know if that goes for the other 49 States, or not?) "*Southern California* is the 'bank robbery *capital of the world*,'" and then he added, "A LACSD (Los Angeles County Sheriff Department) deputy told me that the biggest bank robbery in the whole United States was right here in good ole sunny southern California and it was for $437,000.00."

He continued, "Also, the most bullets ever fired during a bank robbery was here in North Hollywood (The Valley) with 2,000 rounds (bullets) fired on February 28, 1997."

"Also, in 1992 east of L. A, out in the I. E. (Inland Empire), just off of the 91 and 15 Freeway (the Highway to 'lost' wages as I call it, Las Vegas) 1980, 33 police vehicles were either damaged and/or completely destroyed during a bank robbery of Bank of America's Norco branch."

"An FBI agent told me that bank robberies in the United States rose 71% (and that's a lot, folks) and the agent in charge also told me that there were 28 bank robberies in 1992 in just one single day."

Charlie added some more bank robbery information for Sarge's benefit, "The police code in L. A. for a bank robbery is Penal Code, 211 PC. And some of the reasons that the crooked and lowlife bank robbers love to do their 'dirty' business in Los Angeles, is that we have 1,000 miles of freeways."

And also, "We have six million cars on the roads and highways here, and17 million people going here and yonder. Also, we have 10,000 square miles for them to hide in right after they make their score.

"Some of the most famous, or infamous actually were, the 'Yankee' bandit around 1983 in the downtown area of L. A. He hit six banks, all Bank of America branches, he must love B of A."

"And his take was $13,197.00 for all six branches. Also 25% of all bank robberies were close to our old and historic, City Hall." The advent of 'Retail Banking' was a big draw to the bank robbers in and around Los Angeles and southern California.

In 1983 a very bad guy bank robber named Eddie Dodson, a coke head clean out of control, was the one who got the biggest ever take of $437,000.00. Also, there was a bank robber in the 1990s whose nickname was 'Casper' (like in the Casper the Ghost), he was a member of the infamous *Rolling-sixties* (Blue bandanas) *Crips street gang*.

'Casper' read about the huge pay-day of $437,000.00 and decided that he and some of his 'homies' could do the same thing. And they did, the hit dozens of banks over a five- year period of time until they got caught because one of the homeboys got high on Meth and told his girlfriend who was robbing all of those banks.

Now back to the action; Charlie said to Sarge, "Now you know a lot about bank robberies that you did not know before, right my *niño*?" Then added, "You do not have quite as many bank robberies out there in Orange County as they do here in L. A. but you do have several, right?"

Captain Danks told Charlie in a very *urgent* voice, "Two days ago the Bank of America branch located at Hollywood and Cahuenga (just down the street from the corner of '*Hollywood and Vine*') as well as the famous round Capital Records office building, the crooks took away $50,000.00 in used/worn-out 'Dead President' (e.g. large bills). Those paper notes are completely untraceable and yet, still usable."

And then he continued, "Yesterday, the Bank of America office at Wilshire and Harvard (in the tall Travelers Insurance building) just west of downtown L. A. was also robbed and it was a very volatile situation for a while, then the bad guys got away with about $75,000.00 in *Ben Franklin's* $100.00 dollar bills and *Ulysses Grant's* $50.00 dollar bills."

"Thank *God* nobody was hurt, the bank staff and the innocent customers were just very, very shaken-up. Now today, just fifteen *minutes* ago, the Bank of America branch at sixth and Alvarado, right by the famous little old lake at *MacArthur Park*."

The park was named after the famous World War II hero *Douglas MacArthur*, one of country's greatest Generals, according to Charlie. He still likes to visit the park every now and then when he is in the infamous 'Rampart Division' of the LAPD.

Charlie's beloved mama*, Vivian Lee Dickinson*, used to take him to this park and out on the lovely little lake when he was just a wee little Irish lad. There were not many Irish in L. A. back in the day, but Charlie's wonderful mom and hard-working and equally hard-drinking, dad, were some of the few in this area at that time.

More now from the Cap, he was very stressed out due to his worry that soon one of these meth-head bank robbers was going to kill someone, or several innocent persons.

He continued and he had Charlie's completely-undivided attention, "They only got $25,000.00, in twenty-dollar bills, as that was a small office and in a not so wealthy neighborhood and they did not have any $50's or $100's at the tellers windows."

"Charlie," he said really loudly, "I need *you*, and my outstanding Sargent *Hernandez*, to get right on this situation, like *yesterday*, and stay on it 24/7 just like white on rice, and I need you to bring the whole *world* of law enforcement in L. A. down on the heads of these deplorable criminals."

Charlie finally got a chance to ask a question of the Cap, "Sir, do you want us to use what some might say is 'excessive force' in order to save a lot of lives?" Captain Danks *immediately* replied,

"When you find them, and I know you two will, bring the 'wrath' of God down upon their heads."

^^^^^

Charlie told Sarge what his *other* boss had just told him. And within 60 seconds, Charlie had pulled over to the side of the road of the *Pasadena* Freeway, almost ran into a roving taco food van, and two other cars. Sarge then said, "Relax Jefe, you are going to get us *totaled* out, if you do not slow down, just a little bit."

Charlie, retorted, "Sarge, that 'Taco Truck' just made me hungry for some good Mexican food, I love Mexico and also Mexican food, you know what I mean." Sarge just *ignored* him, and pulled his seat belt tighter, and said a little prayer that he survives this trip back to L. A.

Charlie hit his speed dial list for, Jan Smoker, Howard Wallace, Sergeant Kevin Lybrand (OCSD), Brett and Bailey Long and told them all, "Let the *games* begin, bring everything you've got, we are going to have to get *'down and dirty'* and work day and night, to catch these low lives before they injure or kill someone (s)."

Just as old Charlie clicked off his cell phone, and got ready to punch his hot BMW 750 iL with a 'M' rated *engine*, it rang almost immediately. Calling was *Tom Jones, (*No not the fabulous *Irish singer still singing in Las Vegas)* a good friend and *fellow* PI (or *Private Detective,* he preferred to be called) who lived and worked out of his very large and lovely home in Newport Beach, California.

Tom was a *world* traveling PI and had worked for the CIA, and the FBI at one time. He had also worked on several other criminal and white-collar investigations with Charlie and Sarge.

He was an excellent, as well as a very articulate public speaker, therefore, Charlie had him talk to the *news media* whenever that was necessary in a case. Tom was from the mid-west and he had that very likeable personality that folks from that part of our country generally have.

Also, he was exceptionally well read, and knowledgeable about current events in the U. S. and also one of Charlie's favorite places to visit, Israel. He also is a History buff, and has seen most of the popular movies made in Hollywood.

Charlie had left Tom a message to get back to him asap, and as usual, he did. Don is very dependable and Charlie has asked for his kind assistance on several criminal investigations previously.

Then after they finished their short, very short, conversation, he said to Sarge, "They are all coming now, good luck to the bad boys (and girls), you are going to need it. Charlie's A-Team is coming and they're coming your way."

"You can run, you can hide, you can lay-low, you can move clear across the globe, but you cannot, you absolutely cannot avoid being hunted down by us, like the animals that you are."

Charlie likes to say the same sort of thing, except he says, "We will hunt you down, we will find you, we will hurt you (no excessive force, of course); and then my A-*Team* and I, we will take-you-down!"

Charlie loves **John Walsh's** (*America's Most Wanted*) T V Show, he really does. Also, Charlie likes to quote John's famous line, "I am out there chasing the bad guys, and I will *not* waiver, I will *not* delay, and I will *not* quit, until I find them, arrest them, and put them in some dark dank freezing cold or burning hot, prison."

Charlie used to watch 'America's Most Wanted' with his two *excellent* sons, when they were young, they are now very successful Law Enforcement Officers in Orange County. They just loved the show and watched it every week with their old man.

The great TV show ran from 1988 to about 2011 and it was one of the longest running TV shows ever on television. It ran for 25 TV seasons, or 23 years. And a quite interesting and little-known fact is that John Walsh was not the first choice for the starring role.

The famous mystery author and retired cop, *Joseph Wambaugh* was the first choice, however, he turned down the role as he felt that it would not last a year. After he declined, another man was selected.

That man's name was *Rudolf 'Rudy' Giuliani*, little known at the time, however it just so happens that today in 2020, he is **President Donald Trump's** *personal attorney.*

Ray Felherrer is a retired *Satie* (New Jersey Highway Patrol, as well as a Special 'Robbery and Homicide' Detective for the Newark Police Department). He is tough as they come and he has more street smarts than any *cop* from the east coast that Charlie ever met.

Charlie really liked Ray he truly did. Ray had a great personality, and he always had a funny joke to tell people to help brighten up their days. He is older now, just like our man Charlie, however, he can still investigate and solve criminal activities whenever Charlie asks for his help. He still loves law enforcement, he truly does.

Ray's very smart, tall and nice-looking wife, Judy is a retired 'Security Chief' from a huge senior-citizen retirement community in Laguna Beach, southern California. She was responsible for the health and safety of 18,000 plus senior citizen residents.

Judy was always the first officer to respond to any calls where an elderly resident was being harassed or bothered by a non-resident, a flaky attorney and/or a suspicious looking man. She was quite brave and professional in her duties.

Next was, Ron Edwards a former engineer in upstate New York and in charge of the power grid for thousands of acres and millions of homes. Charlie asked him to provide portable generators for their temporary A-Team headquarters and also for any night-time raids and/or arrests.

He was a very nice man, and just like Charlie he loved cats. He and *Peggy*, his wife have two absolutely adorable kittens, albeit, they are full of mischief and high energy.

Peggy, Ron's wife, was an excellent public speaker as well as a very accomplished author and editor. She was picked by Charlie to assist with the handling of press releases and news media requests, as well as Facebook, twitter and social media reports.

Because the whole city was worried about the bank robbers running wild in L. A. there was a lot of news coverage, and the good Mayor picked Charlie to handle that for him, as his PR (public relation) department was buried with other problems and key issues.

Sue Herbert is very sharp and also has a background in law enforcement. She was once an OCSD deputy in charge of the Laguna Woods Village community. She kept all of the elderly senior citizens Safe and Sound and worked 24/7 on many occasions.

Chuck, who is Sue's fiancé, was a former 'navy Seal' and underwater expert. Charlie's A-Team may very well need his expertise since LA is very close to the lovely and majestic royal-blue Pacific Ocean.

Charlie told Sarge, "This is our *updated* A-Team list, and I want you to text it to the **LASD** Sheriff, and **LAPD**, Administration, so they know what's what, and what's going down- out here in Central L. A. (The City of the Angels):

1. Jan Smoker, Chief in House and Office Investigator

2. Howard Wallace, First V.P. and Charlie's Black Op's Team Supervisor.

3. Captain David Alan, Brea PD, Coordinator with all National Law Enforcement.

4. Angie Quomri, International GPS (Global Positing Satellite) Technician.

5. Brett Long, Logistics and Locations Manager
6. Bailey Long, Computer Software Investigations Manager
7. Ray Feldherrer, Protection and Body-Guard Specialist
8. Tim Dupuie, Military, and Street Uniforms, for Charlies whole A-Team.
9. Ron Edwards, Vehicle and Procurement Specialist
10. Peggy Edwards, Police Radio (OCSD, LAPD and LCSD) Monitor.
11. Kevin Lybrand, OCSD, Weapons and Armory Specialist.
12. Sue Herbert, Insurance Coordinator with insurance companies
13. Chuck (Sue's fiancée), Forced Entry Specialist and Demolition Expert

Charlies A-Team Advisers:

1. Great City of Los Angeles, Eric Garcetti, Mayor
2. LA Sheriff Chief Coroner, Alex Villanueva, Sheriff
3. LA Police Chief, Michael Moore, Chief
4. OCDA Todd Spitzer, District Attorney
5. OCSD Don Barnes, Sheriff
6. RCSD Chad Bianco, Sheriff

Sometimes Charlie likes to call his A-Team, 'the **Band'** for short, and also to confuse the criminals who are monitoring the LAPD, and the LASD, radio calls. It is well known that the crooks frequently listen in on law enforcement calls.

Then Charlie added, "Sarge, my *niño*, as you can plainly see, we have the finest Investigation and Apprehension (I and A) team in the whole state, and more than likely, the whole country. We truly do."

Sarge noticed that Charlie was deep in thought, whatever that may be for the old guy, and then his BFF and *Jefe* spoke these words, "A quick question for you my son, what do you want to do when we nab these deplorable bank robbers who intimidate and scare innocent women, children and older men?"

Sarge did not respond right away, as he could tell that Charlie wanted to say more. Charlie did, and this is what he added, "I bet you want to get promoted to Captain Danks job as I 'heard it through the *Grape Vine'* that he was being promoted to be the new 'Under-Sheriff (Assistant Sheriff) for the whole OCSD department."

Sarge really enjoyed working for the Cap and feels that Jason has taught him a lot about *"Community Policing,"* and also law enforcement as well, and also his wife the lovely LT Yvette 'Marie' Murrieta, really liked him as a boss also.

Sarge did not expect that deep a question from Charlie, as he dearly loved the old man, but found him to be more of a non-intellectual for the most part. He pondered and then pondered some more.

He finally replied to Charlie, "My Jefe, no, what I really want to do, is take early retirement from the OCSD. I've done my twenty as you know, so that I can spend more time with my lovely Señora Murrieta, and her family as well as my own."

Then he took a breath, and continued, "Like you, boss, I have had to work long hours, very long hours, and also work 24/7, on several occasions, and I have not had the time to do the things with the my *marvelous* wife and my family and friends that I wanted to do."

More from Sarge, "As a matter of fact, my fearless leader, as soon as I help you capture these bad guys, I am telling the Captain that I am 'hanging-up' my *guns* and heading off-into *the Sunset*, to Mexico and far beyond, with *my* girl."

CHAPTER FOUR

CHARLIE'S SECURE SATELLITE CELL PHONE rang, and as always it rang to *"Private Eyes"*, of course, what else would a real-life private eye have for a ring tone? Charlie always loved *"Hall and Oates"* the fantastic singing/songwriting duo from *Philly*!

"I see you, you see me, watch you blowin' in the wind, when you're making a scene, oh, girl, you've got to know, what my head overlooks, the senses will show to my heart, when it's watching for lies, you can't escape my *Private Eyes*." On the ring tone were these words:

"You play with words, you play with love, you can twist it all around, baby, that ain't enough 'Cos girl, I'm gonna know if you're letting me in or letting me go, don't lie, when you're hurting inside 'Cos you can't escape my Private Eyes."

[Written by: Daryl Hall, Janna Allen, Sara Allen (Halls girlfriend), and Warren Pash, 1981].

Charlie just loves that tune, he really does. He also loves Philadelphia, and he calls his gorgeous model wife, his Philly girl.

The marvelous duo, was comprised of John Hall and Daryl Oates, both especially gifted and 'genius' singer/songwriters.

Daryl Hall said he likens their duo to *Mick Jagger* and Ron Wood, one of the best rock n' roll bands in history, the *'Rolling Stones'*.

Charlie says that the *Beatles* were the best, but Sarge and Yvette say the 'Stones' were better.

On the other end of the phone was *Don Barnes*, the OCSD Sheriff and Chief Coroner. He was just checking in with Charlie and Sarge and wanted to know what kind of condition our condition was in with regard to our investigation.

Charlie responded to the Sheriff, "Sadly, Sheriff, we have not taken down the bank- robbery gang yet, but trust me Sir, Sarge and our A-Team, and I shall, and you can take that to the bank."

Just as soon as Charlie got off of the phone with the good Sheriff, *'Private Eyes'* began singing to him once again. It was Captain Danks, Sarge and Yvette's boss at the OCSD on Santa Ana Street, in Santa Ana.

The Cap wanted to know the same thing as did the Sheriff and he got the same answer from Charlie, that is to say, "Nothing yet Captain, but I will definitely keep you posted, rest assured of that."

Charlie just had a thought, a brainstorm as it were in his opinion anyway, he decided to call the excellent RCSD (Riverside County Sheriff and Coroner), *Chad Bianco*. He and the good Sheriff had worked on several criminal cases in the past. And Charlie held him in high regard.

Charlie spoke just as soon as the Sheriff answered his personal cell phone, "Sheriff I was wondering if I could borrow one of your good deputies, perhaps a weapons expert, to assist us with our nightmare bank-robbery investigation?"

Sheriff Bianco, replied immediately, "I've heard and read about the heinous bank robberies in L.A. It is very high profile out here in the I.E. (*Inland Empire*) because we are right next door to L. A. County."

Then he hesitated, then he continued, "Of course, anything for my old P.I. *compadre*. And I will let you have my undersheriff for up to six months, he is the best man that I got amigo, how about that?"

Charlie was shocked, he really was, then after he gained his composer, somewhat, he said, "Sheriff I cannot thank you and the RCSD enough, and I shall return the huge favor sometime in the future when you need a hand with one of your investigations."

Charlie was still feeling great about getting another very qualified member on his A-Team Investigation unit, and he was having a 'donut' and milk, he does not drink coffee anymore, he told Sarge that it causes GERD (severe stomach problems).

He also told Sarge, "You know my son, everybody needs milk. You and Yvette and your whole family should be drinking milk every day. Look at how healthy I am and I have been drinking lots of milk my whole life. But I still like a good cold Coke or Pepsi Cola every now and then."

Then just before he took his first bite of a French Curler (or his *Chocolate* Long John or his jelly-filled glazed donut) his cell rang once again, it was *'Sergeant Kevin Lybrand'* and he was calling his man Charlie to get an update on their investigation.

Charlie very quickly took a bite, a big bite of the cruller, and a big gulp of milk and replied, "Hey Kevin, what's happening my friend?" Then he added, "Kevin I am right in the middle of an important phone call, can I get right back to you after I finish my three donuts, oops, oh, I mean my long distant phone call?"

Kevin, laughed and then laughed some more, then almost gagged with *laughter* and then finally spoke, "Charlie ole man, go right ahead and finish your three donuts, oops, oh no, I mean your important phone call, and then call me back, OK?"

Kevin related to Charlie that he had just been to the exotic and very old China town. Charlie loved Chinese food and ate it whenever he had the opportunity, and he and his lovely *long-legged* beautiful wife, went there several times every year.

Kevin added, "I just talked to *Hong Kong* 'Triade' gang members, scary, very scary individuals with lots of tat's (Tattoo's), all over their bodies as well as their faces and on top of their shaved heads."

More from Kevin, "They told me, since I was from the *barrio* in Anaheim, a sister city of L. A, that they were not involved in the robberies at all, bank robberies were not their thing, but they heard some *'rumblings'* on the street (heard it from the grape vine) that some bad, and he said very bad again, *Russian Mafia* types were throwing around a lot of cash, *Ben Franklins* ($100.00 bills) and U. S. *Grants* ($50.00 bills)."

He then added, "The leader of the gang, which had five members, was named '**Vicktor Karchenco**' and he was big, and he was vicious and, he was most definitely deadly." Then he thought for a second, and added some more:

The five vicious and quite violent gang members were named:

1. Alexandar (Alex) Kopiyka: Vicktor's Lieutenant, and a weapons expert

2. 'Big' Boris Omsk Tvershaya: a mixed martial arts, & hand-to-hand combat expert

3. Oleg Georgi Kalmanovich: the body guard and look out-man

4. Nikoli Mironov Syeryozha. The 'enforcer,' he was more deadly than a rattlesnake

[Charlie absolutely hates, really hates, snakes of any kind]

5. Vladimir Yelchin Alexievich: The get-away driver as well as the R and R man

His nickname was the '**Fisherman**,' and the reason for that name was that if you cheated him, or disrespected him, or if he just did not like the way you looked, 'he would put you to *sleep* with the fish.'

Then Kevin asked Charlie, "Do you remember the_*God Father* movies, Charlie?" And Charlie replied, "Yes, Kev I saw all of them, actually several times." Then Charlie said, "Good work Sergeant Lybrand, very good work. You just got us our first concrete lead on the bank robbers."

Then, "Hit some hot spots while you are still there in Chinatown and turn-over some rocks and see if any low life illegal Ruskies (or *Commie Pinkos,* as I like to call them) turn up. Remember Kevin, '*head on a swivel*,' like Sarge always says."

After Kevin's call, and taking some, or a lot, of his stomach medicine for his GERD, Charlie called Sarge. He was down in Korea Town, around *Pico and Alvarado* area. Charlie told Sarge that he loved Korean people as they were almost always very honest and honorable individuals. However, "Just 'sniff' around a little bit and see if anything, or anyone, *'smells.'*"

Sarge quickly responded, "10-4 Jefe, you know that I am on the job, and remember old man, be careful out there and watch your back." Sarge loved our man Charlie but he just could not help himself teasing him every chance he got.

Then Sarge thought, and decided to add, "Charlie, old man, sometime let's, you, Yvette 'Marie', your lovely wife, Lynn, Kevin and his wife, and Captain Danks and his wife, all get together and fly down to my and your favorite place, Ensenada, Mexico."

And, he also stated, "And, *Jefe*, we could all sing *'Kum ba Yah'* on the way down there. And eat a ton of excellent real Mexican food (comida) on the jet plane. Also, you could tell us some of your well known 'war stories." Then he laughed, again.

Later that same day, Charlie caught a call from **Billy Thieme,** an old friend who lives out in the Valley (San Fernando Valley). He used to work for the LACSD (Department) in the 'rough and tumble' *Firestone Division* in the Norwalk, Dairy Valley, Hawaiian Gardens, and Bell Gardens.

Charlie was working at that time for the LAPD and he and Billy had done some 'door-kicking' together back in the day. Billy told Charlie that he eats at a wonderful Jewish delicatessen in North Hollywood.

And the name was 'The World-Famous Cantor's Deli,' and added that their hot *pastrami sandwich* would just melt in your mouth, it really would, Billy repeated. Charlie had 'broken bread' with Billy at that delicious Deli before and he absolutely loved their pastrami plate with coleslaw and a big kosher dell pickle.

But then again, Charlie our famous foodie, loved almost everything in that place, he really did. Billy told Charlie that there was a well-known Russian restaurant and sports club and bar, right next door to the deli.

Charlie knew that there was a very large *Russian enclave* who lives in and around North Hollywood. Most of them were here legally and they came to the U.S. to get away from the Godless *Communists*, however, lots were not, and they were former FSB [KGB], same people, same faces, just a different name.

The restaurant's name was the *'Little Odessa's* Russian Community Lounge.' Billy knew some Russian friends who frequented that place. His friends overheard some tough and nasty looking guys in the corner one night.

According to Billy's friend, the leader of the 'pack' was a scary, very scary, looking man named 'Vicktor Kharchenko,' and he was a cousin of the very infamous *'Decebal Stefan Emilian Matasareno'* half of the North Hollywood 'Shoot Out' meth-head duo back in the 1990's. Stefan was half Russian and half Albanian.

The other half of the quite deadly duo was *"Larry Eugene 'Gene' Phillips*, Jr." He was born in the United States, but he loved European women and cars. Also, he was a gym 'rat' and that is where he met Stefan. That was at *'Golds' gym* out in the Simi Valley.

Gene was very strong however, but not very big, and on the other hand, Stefan was a huge monster. He was 6'6" and 350 pounds, mostly just *fatty* tissue. His mind was much smaller than his body, much smaller.

And it just so happens that he was one of the infamous meth-head bank robbers back in the 1990's that took down the *Bank of America* branch in North Hollywood. That was the worst *botched* bank robbery in US history.

Charlie turned on his cell phone to the *itune* feature and looked up one of his all- time favorite blues songs, "**Boom, boom**" (boom, boom) by the incredible Mississippi Delta *bluesman, 'Mr. John Lee Hooker.' It started out like this:*

"Boom, boom, boom, boom, I'm gonna' shoot you right down, right off your feet, take you home with me, put you in my house, Boom, boom, boom, boom; Mmmm, Mmmm, Mmmm."

"I love to see you walk, up and down the floor, when you're talking to me, that baby talk, I like it like that. You talk like that, you knock me dead, right off of my feet, a Haw, haw, haw, Whoa!"

(Produced by the famous Stan Lewis, for Vee Jay Records, Written by John Lee Hooker, off of his 'Burnin' album, 1962.)

^^^^^

John wrote this mega hit back in the day, in 1962 for Vee Jay Records. Also, Charlie told Sarge and Yvette 'Marie,' that John was inducted into the Rock n' Roll Hall of Fame in 1995. Lt Yvette really loved the Blues and so did Sarge.

The quite famous English rock band, the *'Animals'* covered John's fabulous song and their version was done in1964 (British Invasion). It also was a huge hit for them as well.

Then our man Charlie called Jan Smoker, and asked her to call her old CIA friends and see what they could find out about our 'Fisherman' and his Crew. Jan is so fast and efficient, that she called Charlie back in only four hours.

She started out by saying, "Charlie my good *Hijo*, my CIA contacts at the *'Agency'* said that the *Fisherman* and all five of his evil cohorts, were all former FSB (formerly known as the KGB) members.

The same mean and violent type people, same scary looking faces, same snake-like whisper voices, but just different names." And then she looked at her notes, and started speaking again, "These are bad dudes, real bad dudes, Charles, so 'keep your head on a swivel' as Sarge likes to say."

Charlie was shocked at how much Jan found out in so little time, he replied, "Thank you ever so much Jan, very important news from your voice to my ears. And remember careful is my middle name."

Jan laughed, and laughed, and laughed then answered, "Sure, Charlie, sure you will, old man." Then Jan had a big smile on her face, and hung up her secure cell phone.

ALL ABOUT OUR MAN CHARLIE THE PI:

Charles Warner Kennedy (Charlie) O'Brien, *is a Dreamer,* he truly is and he has been a dreamer ever since he was a little kid in rural Ojai (now, Tennis County) California.

He was born in downtown Los Angeles, in what is now called 'Korea Town', then his parents moved Ojai, and after that he grew up in a *barrio* in La Puente and El Monte (San Gabriel Valley), California.

Charlie lived with and went to school with several serious 'gangbangers.' Since they knew him from a kid, they did not stab or shoot him like they did the other *Anglo* (white) kids.

He, to this very day loves Latino people, he really does. He told Sarge, "I am part Latino inside did you know?" He thinks Latina women are quite striking with lovely long dark hair and mysterious dark eyes.

Sadly, Charlie did not grow up in a wholesome home. Actually, it was quite dysfunctional, and his father was a drunk, a mean drunk, that is the worst kind. But at least he was a working *alcoholic* and Charlie always had 'three hots and a cot,' as convicts say.

Charlie found out, not too long before his dad passed away, that he had been a good person when he was young and did not drink much at all, back when he was a kid growing up in Iowa.

His mother was a wonderful and caring woman but her father, just like Charlie's dad, was an alcoholic as well. Charlie has been to the old Homestead in Iowa, and just loved it, it sits on 160 acers of land.

He considers himself a third *Latino* because of being from the 'hood' (neighborhood). He just loves Latin people as well as the wonderful country of Mexico, which he has visited many, many times.

Charlie always tells people that they make the best souvenirs and handmade gifts in Tijuana, Ensenada, and the other border towns. He buys tons of neat hand- made stuff to give as gifts every time he goes there.

When he was small, he wanted to be a 'cowboy' like *Hopalong Cassidy* (Hoppy), or the *Lone Ranger*, the *Cisco Kid*, among many other of his cowboy hero's.

Then as a teenager he fell in love with the *'noir genre'* of police detectives, private eyes, and private investigators. Such as *Mike Hammer*, *Sam Spade*, *Magnum* PI, Harry "*Dirty Harry*" Callahan (e.g. Clint Eastwood).

And also, The A-*Team*, *Columbo*, 77 *Sunset* Strip, *Route* 66, *Horatio* Caine, Miami Vice, *Cannon*, Nick *Carter*, Sherlock *Holmes*, *Kojak*, and the greatest lawyer of all time, *Perry Mason*.

Also, he watched and admired Hercule Poirot, Ellery Queen, Jim Rockford, and Spenser, among many, many other great detective and mystery TV shows that Charlie watched while he was growing up.

Now days, he dreams that he is Jason Strathan, Liam Neeson, Clint Eastwood, Duane 'The Rock' Johnson, Chris Hemsworth, Kurt Russell, Jackie Chan, or Arnold Schwarzenegger, depending upon the current dream he is having at any particular time.

Charlie the Private Investigator is described as follows: first and foremost, a good and kind man, albeit, he is the first to admit that he is not perfect nor all together, at all.

Charlie is one of the few, true-life *fearless detectives* in America or so I have been told. He uses his personal and extensive experience which is based upon his solid daily work ethic and personal beliefs--as well as his background of a twenty- year career with the LAPD (the excellent as well as outstanding, Los Angeles Police Department). The LAPD is known and respected all around the world just as the OCSD.

He worked under the great Barnard 'Bernie' *Parks*, one of the *best* police chiefs ever in LA, next to *William 'Bill' Parker* (who the city named the Police Headquarters building after), *and* Charles 'Charlie' *Beck*, also one of the most outstanding Chiefs LA ever has had, of course.

He was a 'Robbery and Homicide Detective' and he worked on the demonic possessed 'Charlie Manson' family case. As well as many other very high-profile murder cases in LA (Los Angeles). The *madman* and demon-*possessed* Charlie Manson just died recently in prison after being locked up for the past 40 years.

Our man, the good *Charlie* always said that it was too bad that the state of California did away with the death penalty given to Manson (which he fully deserved) for the brutal and senseless killing of several people back in Hollywood in 1969.

Some of the victims were the famous and beautiful actress *Sharon Tate* (and her precious and unborn baby) who was married to international movie producer, *Roman Polanski*. Also, there was *Jay Sebring*, a well know Hollywood hairstylist.

These experiences combined with his current ten years of being a PI (Private Investigator, or Private Eye as some prefer to call him), gave him the innate ability to investigate and then solve, very large *'White Collar'* crimes as well as heinous *'Criminal'* cases in the USA as well as all over the globe.

He finds that by putting his beliefs into action (putting his feet where his mouth is...so to speak) it gives him an edge in understanding, dealing with, and then capturing heinous crooks *and* criminals of all kinds.

Charlie primarily investigates embezzlement cases in the so called *'too big to fail'* banks in the good ole US of A, as well as in foreign countries located all around the world.

He also investigates serious criminal activities, as in *'Ponzi' schemes* (think Bernard L. **'Bernie' Madoff** and his 65 Billion...yes *Billion* dollar rip off of the American public) and also unethical stockbroker/investment bankers (Lehman Brothers, AGI, Manhattan Bank, the Old Merrill Lynch Corporation (now owned and operated by Bank of America).

And one of the 'worst of the worst', *Country Wide Funding* (which was located in the real estate capital of the world, California), the list sadly goes on forever.

Charlie wants to find the executives from these evil, and corrupt banks and money market funds, and security-broker organizations and put them in a *black-*ops prison in Europe, or southeast Asia.

He also sometimes helps to solve other types of 'criminal' activities that occur in his beloved California, where he hangs his hat (lives). Some of these crimes include bank art theft robberies, kidnappings, crooked *politician's* shenanigans, and bombings, just to name a few.

During Charlie's in-depth investigations as a PI, he frequently encounters some very scary *villains* and heinous and extremely dangerous *criminals*.

He uses his strong and honest beliefs, his devotion to duty, as well as relying on his very sharp mind to assist him in researching and then solving, his very challenging, and complicated, and usually quite dangerous cases.

Charles, albeit, his best friends, fellow Private Investigators (Private Eyes), and LAPD (Los Angeles Police Department) detectives, and the OCSD (Orange County Sheriff's Department), just call him **Charlie**. I want you to know that Charlie does *not* enjoy getting older.

As a matter of fact, he hates it... immensely. He truly does. People tell him, “Charlie, you look good for your age.” Kind of a left-handed compliment would you not say?

He realizes that they are just trying to be kind, however, he wishes that instead, they would say to him: “Charlie, you're still tall, dark, and handsome.”

That would be a big lie but he could whole-heartedly buy into it. He really could. And, besides, he is still tall, and one-out-of-three isn't bad, right?

He tries and tries, but he just cannot stop good old *father-time* from marching across his handsome (he wishes) face. In addition, most of his previously nice dark almost black, hair is now rapidly turning gray. But he always says, "At least I still have all of my hair, *thank God*!"

A lot of his friends are bald and they would kill to have gray hair rather than have no hair at all. Oh, well, we all have our crosses to bear in this crazy old world and his currently is that he just does not have the looks, nor the energy, that he did when he was in his prime.

Charlie now lives in Beverly Hills, California (just west of downtown Los Angeles) which some people call "La-La Land." They are incorrect though, LA is "the City of Angels" ...it is *'Hollywood'* that is really called La-La Land, trust me on that.

He was born and raised here and he most likely will die here...maybe one day soon...you just never know when you will be run over by a big RTD bus or a 400 horse power Dodge Charger (OCSD or a LAPD, police cruiser) chasing a gangbanger in a stolen Mercedes Benz 500S; or even worse, hit by one of the new red-blue-yellow train lines now crisscrossing LA like a scrabble board (or falling dominos).

He actually lives in *Beverly Hills*, California, very close to the majestic and royal blue *Pacific* Ocean. That lovely and one of the most expensive cities in the world to live in, is located in the United States, and is close to the famous city of *Huntington* Beach (*Surf City*, USA).

Remember the *Beach Boys*? Some of them recently performed at the LWV Performing Arts Center. Charlie was told by some residents that it was just an absolutely fabulous concert, it really was!

CHAPTER FIVE

ON WEEKENDS CHARLIE DRIVES HIS CLASSIC 1964 Chevy Impala two-door hardtop. This beautiful ride has been completely restored to the original condition. He just loves classic cars and he has owned several of them over his life time.

He and his lovely wife like to drive it on Sundays down to Lovely Laguna Beach, sometimes, as well as cruise around L.A. just for fun. Lots of people give him a 'big smile' when they see him and his wife go by. And Charlie always smiles, and says, "Right back at you my friend".

His Impala is the Super Sport model with a large big-block 409 cubic inch V-8 HO (high output) *engine*, 4 on the floor stick *transmission* with a deluxe chrome-knob shifter. It also has Posi-traction non-slip rear end differential and original *Cragar magnesium* wheels from the 1960s.

It has very large and comfortable black- leather bucket seats and it is original deep maroon in color. The engine is all chrome as well as the whole undercarriage.

The whole car is in pristine and mint condition, it truly is. It appraised for around $75,000 recently, however, Charlie would never sell his baby. It is part of his persona and makes him feel young once again whenever he takes it for a spin.

Every time Charlie drives his baby around LA or the OC on weekends all of the old guys and gals, and even lots of young people give him a thumbs up. Sometimes they even say, "Old guys with old cars Rule." Charlie loves to hear that, he really does.

Charlie liked that comment so much that he went out and had several T-shirts made with that saying printed on the back of them. He does not like T's with writing on the front, just on the back for some unknown reason. Some of them are navy blue but most of them are white, naturally.

Also, he has some T-shirts that say, on the back naturally, ‘Ride high or death,’ and ‘He is not done with me yet, check back with me later’, and ‘Charlie’s Coming, and coming soon.’

The other day as Charlie dressed for work, he *looked* into the *mirror*. Staring back at him was an extremely handsome angular man, around six-feet-four with a surfer mop of Pacific Ocean sun-kissed hair.

He had preternatural hazel eyes...so intense that whenever most women looked at him...they had to avert their eyes in embarrassment.

Well, to be just a bit more truthful, at least his eyes *are* hazel, but hardly any women stared at him any longer. He took *another* look, just for fun, and he saw a good-looking man with an angular face topped by a nest of naturally wavy- black and white (graying) hair.

And he saw a shy smile, albeit Charlie is anything but shy, but his shy smile made women *swoon*...so boyish and charming, yet masculine at the same time. Charlie you dreamer you!

He had a *six-pack* courtesy of crunches and weight lifting at 24 Hour Fitness and a very strict eating regimen. Then, suddenly he realized that he was just *imagining* what he saw in the little mirror.

So, he decided to take *another* look...a harder look this time and he saw his real self, he thought anyway.

Appearing in his mirror was a very nice looking, *mature* gentleman with a full head of hair, albeit some of it was graying, well, all right, a lot of it.

He saw friendly-warm yet piercing *hazel* eyes, that sometimes looked blue, other times looked green (Irish eyes are shining) and sometimes even looked brown.

He did not see a six-pack this time around (frown) nor a smile that would make women swoon, sorry Charlie, but you have to know your limitations I am sorry to tell you.

All-in-all, what he saw this time was a man who had lived a very hard life, always worked hard, always, and tried to help others who were less fortunate than himself, and always tried to do his best at whatever tasks laid before him.

Then, he said to himself out loud as usual, "Charlie, you're the man!" Then, he turned and left the bathroom with the image of the *first* man he saw in the mirror, still in his mind's eye.

Do you remember that great old 'Motown' song, "Charlie Brown" by the fabulous *Coasters*? Charlie just absolutely loves Barry Gordy's *Motown* Music, he truly does.

Charlie and his lovely, model-looking-like wife, Lynn, just saw the fabulous *'Smokey Robinson'* at the Cerritos, quite a marvelous *venue* Charlie says, “Performing Arts Center in southern California.”

It was just an unbelievable performance and just to make it even more memorable, Mr. Barry Gordy (yes, *the man himself*) was in the audience. How cool is that? Smokey and Barry live in the same theater. Wow.

Do you remember some of the fun lyrics, "Charlie Brown who walks into the classroom real cool and slow and calls the English teacher Daddy-O. And why's everybody always pickin' on me?"

"Who's always goofing in the hall, guess who? Yeah, you, Charlie Brown." This amongst tons of other great Motown songs, was written by Mike *Stoller* and Jerry *Leiber*, two of the great Rock and Roll songwriters of all time, in Charlie's mind.

Well Charlie has a great sense of humor, he got it from his beloved mama, Vivian Lee Martin. He loves to laugh and he also loves to tell funny stories, and sometimes they are true, sometimes.

However, some of his fellow Private Detectives, and LACSD, LAPD officers, amongst many others, love to sing, "Here comes *Charlie Brown*" whenever they see him after a long period of time.

Some people say that Charlie is a pessimist, but that is just not true. Actually, he used to be a consummate optimist, but he has never been a pessimist, ever.

‘A glass half-full’ kind of guy as they say, however, that was before all of the many 'trials and tribulations' in his life. Also, no, he has said my glass is almost empty.

Now days, he says, "my glass is half-full and half-empty". That is how the realist looks at things in this crazy, old, mixed- up world that we live in. Life has a way of changing one's perspective on one's life over time, does it not?

In addition, our man Charlie likes things simple, real, simple and the simpler the better. He subscribes to that age old saying(adage): KISS (keep it simple stupid).

Life today is way, way too complicated for him. For one thing, he does not understand computers at all. When he was a kid, they had manual adding machines, and then along came the electric versions.

He used them all of the time and loved them. Even still has some laying around. He also used to be so smart and quick that he did lots of calculations in his head.

He is not exactly sure why, but he cannot do that anymore. Old age, early dementia, perhaps. His cell phone is also somewhat of a mystery to him. It is almost like a tiny, small computer these days.

Someone said to him recently, while on an investigation, not a very nice person by the way, that he was *high*-tech challenged. He would have been quite offended, but he was not sure what they meant. So, he just smiled.

Also, he does not know much about the Internet, nor computer software for that matter. Just the other day he heard that he was on the 'dark web' whatever that is?

Bad he knows, but how did he get there and where is it located? In Europe or the far east?

Charlie is going to call **Jan Smoker** and have her explain to him all about the 'Dark Web' and how to get off of it.

And also find out who put him on it, and then take care of them. She is a wonderful woman, as well as very intelligent, about computers and counter-intelligence.

And the terms and definitions for computers, as well as their software, confuse him greatly. Such as giga-bites, or terra- bites, or thumb drives, RAM, different processors, all-in-ones, and on and on for *Infinium*.

He is planning on taking a computer class from Barbara and Craig, at the LWV PC workshop to understand the 'ins and outs' and nuances of the computer world that the old school private eye finds himself living.

Charlie loves to study his old worn out *Police Manual*, every chance he gets. He truly does. Currently he is studying "Illegal Trespassing" in private senior citizen retirement communities.

The Greek work for 'Blessing' is the word '*eulogia*', which means to benefit from. Charlie can speak a little 'Latin' and some Greek too. Charlie feels that he is blessed above all men with his lovely bride, his lovely home in Laguna Woods Village, and his good friends at the OCSD. These are some benefits that are attached to real life things when you live them day in, and day out, according to Charlie anyway.

ONCE AGAIN, AND OUT OF THE BLUE, Charlie was hailed by his ever present and always within easy reach, cell phone. As you already know, his welcoming ring tone is "Private Eyes" by fantastic Philly boys, Hall and Oates.

On the other end of the line was LT Yvette 'Marie' Murrieta, Charlie's beloved Mija (adopted daughter). He was always so, so very happy whenever she called him, he really was.

She was also known, when not 'on the job' as Mrs. J. J. Hernandez, the Sarge's wonderful and very brave, wife. She was, as you know, a Lieutenant at the Orange County Sheriff's department in the O. C.

Also, Charlie likes to tell everyone, and I do mean everybody, that she is the better half, a much better half, and then he always adds "by far." Whenever anyone tells Sarge what Charlie says, he always responds, "Charlie is right for once in his life, Yvette is the better half, no disagreement on my part about that, none at all."

LT. Yvette was doing some R and R (Research and Reconnaissance) on the *'Fisherman'* his Russki thugs, for the A-Team. And she ran across some very interesting 'dirt' about them and she thought that Charlie would want to hear about it, a-sap.

Yvette spoke as soon as he answered his cell and she said, "Pappy how are you doing? Good I pray, Sarge and I want to have you and Mama Lynn, over for dinner soon, real soon."

"And I will make my famous *tamales*, enchiladas, and burritos, and tacos too. Of course, with Mexican rice, beans, Sarge's BBQ corn, and lots, and lots of hot flour tortillas."

She continued, "Plus as usual, I will make you a big family style taco salad, one of your favorites I know." LT. could almost hear Charlie *salivating* over the phone (he is such a foodie, she thought to herself), so she added quickly, "Calm down Jefe, we got a vicarious bank robbery crime to solve first, then we eat, fiesta, and then eat some more, alright?"

Charlie knows a lot about the OCSD (Orange County Sheriff's Department) and of course, Sarge and LT Yvette work there, however, none of them knew much about the LACSD (Los Angeles County Sheriff's Department), which is one of the largest departments in the United States.

So, one day Yvette 'Marie,' Sarge and Charlie went downtown to visit the LACSD headquarters on Temple Street, in the heart of Los Angeles, right by the historic old City Hall (1930').

There they met with the Sheriff and Chief Coroner (ALEX VILLANUEVA) and also some of his outstanding management team and Watch Commanders.

And.

And this is what the three 'Amigos' (Yvette, Sarge, and Charlie) found out that most of the good and law-abiding citizens of Los Angeles County do not know.

Alex Villanueva, the Sheriff and Chief Coroner, of all of Los Angeles County, which is one of one of the greatest and largest Sheriff's Departments in the whole country, the LASD Department, told Charlie and Sarge and LT Yvette, the brief (very brief) history of his excellent and dedicated department, and this is what he told them:

^^^^^

LOS ANGELES SHERIFF'S DEPARTMENT

The Los Angeles County Sheriff's Department (**LASD**), officially the *County of Los Angeles Sheriff's Department*, is the United States' largest sheriff's department, with approximately 18,000 employees. The department's three main responsibilities entail providing patrol services for 153 unincorporated communities of Los Angeles County, California and 42 cities, providing courthouse security for the Superior Court of Los Angeles County, and the housing and transportation of inmates within the county jail system.

In addition, the department contracts with the Los Angeles Metropolitan Transportation Authority and Metrolink, provides law enforcement services to ten community colleges, patrols over 177 county parks, golf courses, special event venues, two major lakes, 16 hospitals, and over 300 county facilities; and provides services, such as crime laboratories, homicide investigations, and academy training, to smaller law-enforcement agencies within the county.

The Los Angeles County Sheriff's Department's transit division alone is the second largest transit police force in the world, aside from the New York City Police Department.

This is through policing contracts of the Metro trains and buses of the Los Angeles Metro and Metrolink. The Department also contracts with nine campuses of the Los Angeles and Lancaster Community Colleges.

The L.A. County Sheriff's Department's headquarters are located in downtown Los Angeles at the Los Angeles County Hall of Justice.

Personnel

The Los Angeles County Sheriff's Department is the largest sheriff's department and the fourth largest local policing agency in the United States. There are approximately 17,926 employees; over 9,972 sworn deputies and 7,954 non- sworn members (professional staff).

There are an additional 4,200 civilian volunteers, 791 reserve deputies and 400 explorers. On December 3, 2018, **Alex Villanueva** took the oath of office and was sworn in as the 33rd Los Angeles County Sheriff.

LASD deputies provided law enforcement services to over three million residents in an area of 3,171 square miles (8,210 km^2) of the 4,083 square miles on the county, both in the unincorporated county land and within the 42 contract cities.

Organization

The following are the LASD Divisions:

Sheriff's Headquarters

- Undersheriff
  - Sheriff's Information Bureau
- Legal Advisory Unit
- Constitutional Policy Advisors
- Community Outreach

- Strategic Communications
- Chief of Staff
- Legislative Unit
- Audit and Accountability Bureau
- Professional Standards & Training Division
    - Advocacy Unit
    - Internal Affairs Bureau
    - Internal Criminal Investigations Bureau
    - Risk Management Bureau
    - Training Bureau

Administrative Services Division

- Contract Law Enforcement Bureau
- Facilities Planning Bureau
- Facilities Services Bureau
- Financial Programs
- Fiscal Administration
- Personnel Command
    - Personnel Services Bureau
    - Psychological Services Bureau
    - Bureau of Labor Relations and Compliance
- Technology & Support Division
    - Communications & Fleet Management Bureau
    - Data Systems Bureau
    - Records & Identification Bureau
    - Scientific Services Bureau

Custody Operations

Custody Services Division General Population

- Inmate Reception Center
- Men's Central Jail
- Population Management Bureau

- North County Correctional Facility
- Pitchess Detention Center East Facility (Fire Camps)
- Pitchess Detention Center North Facility
- Pitchess Detention Center South Facility

Custody Services Division Specialized Programs

- Century Regional Detention Facility
- Food Services
- Education Based Incarceration / Inmate Services Bureau
- Medical Services Bureau
- Twin Towers Correctional Facility
- Mira Loma Detention Facility

Custody Services Administration Command

- Custody Support Services
- Custody Compliance & Sustainability
- Custody Training & Standards Bureau

Countywide Operations

Countywide Operations Division

- Community Colleges Bureau
- Community Partnerships Bureau
- County Services Bureau
- Parks Bureau (mostly created with the merger with Los Angeles County Office of Public Safety in 2010)

o Court Services Division — Provides security and support services to the Superior.

- Court in the County of Los Angeles. This includes staffing bailiffs, operating courthouse lock-ups, and serving and enforcing civil and criminal process. Court Services provides these services for 48 courthouse locations throughout Los Angeles County, which include the following:
  - Civil Management Bureau
  - Court Services Central
  - Court Services East
  - Court Services West
  - Court Services Transportation Bureau

Special Operations Division

- Aero Bureau
- Special Enforcement Bureau — Special Enforcement Detail (**SWAT**), Canine Services Detail, and Emergency Services Detail (coordinates and participates in mountain search and rescue, underwater search and rescue, and swift water and flood rescue operations)
- Emergency Operations Bureau which includes:
  - Industrial Relations Detail - maintains liaison between the business and labor communities. The Detail also trains patrol personnel in the handling of labor disputes and picket lines.

    Arson Explosives Detail

  - Hazardous Material Detail
  - Transit Services Bureau
  - Los Angeles Metropolitan Transportation Authority

    - Metrolink

- Patrol Operations are divided amongst as follows:
  - North Patrol Division — Lancaster, Malibu/Lost Hills, Palmdale, Santa Clarita Valley, and West Hollywood.
  - South Patrol Division — Carson, Cerritos, Lakewood, Lomita, Norwalk, and Pico Rivera.
  - East Patrol Division — Altadena, La Crescenta Valley, Industry, San Dimas, Temple, and Walnut/Diamond Bar.
  - Central Patrol Division — Avalon, Century, Compton, Marina Del Rey, and South Los Angeles.
- Detective Division — Contains the following; Homicide Bureau, Fraud & Cyber Crimes Bureau, Major Crimes Bureau, Narcotics Bureau, Special Victims Bureau, and the Taskforce for Regional Auto-theft Prevention (T.R.A.P.)

Academy

The Biscaluz Center in Monterey Park, which included the Sheriff's Academy—closed for 30 years—was recently renovated, expanded, and Sheriff's Academy activities moved back there in 2014. Reserves may use either STARS Center or College of the Canyons (Santa Clarita) for academy training. Academy training is 20 weeks long.

Personnel

Many law enforcement agencies throughout Los Angeles County utilize STARS Center and deputy sheriff trainees graduating as deputy sheriffs also undergo detention-specific training. There are separate academy curricula for Deputy Sheriffs, Custody Assistants, Security Officers, and Security Assistants.

County Jail System

The Los Angeles County Sheriff's Department operates the largest jail system in the world. The Los Angeles County Jail provides short-term incarceration services for all of the County (including cities like Los Angeles, Glendale, Burbank, and Long Beach which have their own police departments).

The Men's Central Jail (MCJ) and Twin Towers Correctional Facility (TTCF) are located in a dense cluster northeast of Union Station that is next to the station's rail yard.

The North County Correctional Facility (NCCF) is the largest of the four jail facilities located at the Pitchess Detention Center in Castaic, California. The L.A. County women's jail, called the Century Regional Detention Facility or the Lynwood Jail, is located in Lynwood, California.

Controversies

The Los Angeles County Jail incarcerates about 250,000 serious crime violators and gang individuals each year, and with such large numbers, the jail has faced numerous problems with its facilities.

Following one such controversy, then Los Angeles County Sheriff, **Lee Baca**, announced that the Men's Central Jail could be closed. Construction of a new jail has been proposed to replace the Men's Central Jail.

Another challenge that the Los Angeles County Jail faces is violence within the jail community. Many researchers assert that the violence seen in jails is in part due to males wanting to maintain a position of superiority.

Because those who appear to be weak tend to become victims of sexual violence in jail, some men attempt to demonstrate to others that they are too strong to be taken advantage of.

This level of heightened masculinity is also called hyper-masculinity, and has the potential to manifest itself in the form of violence in a prison setting. Although men prove their masculinity in order to prevent sexual assault, some may also commit sexual assault on others as a mechanism for appearing dominant and masculine.

Related to this issue is Los Angeles County Jail's K6G unit, which is intended to be a separate unit for gay-identified men and transgender women. Although it has been shown that this unit is successful through its lower rates of violence, the creation and systematics of this unit have sparked controversy.

Finally, serious health concerns have begun to arise with the issue of mass incarceration in the Los Angeles County Jails. Several organizations and scholars have analyzed random samples of prisoners with illnesses and the healthcare that they receive while incarcerated.

Although it is generally assumed that many prisoners have antisocial personality disorder, The American Public Health Association claims that some of these prisoners suffer from a variety of other disorders.

They also state that more than 30% of their sample have a severe mental disorder or a substance use disorder. The detainees that were diagnosed with severe mental disorders or substance use were often in jail because they had committed nonviolent crimes.

An issue that arises with the incarceration of individuals with mental disorders is that they must be tested for competency before they can be put on trial, which can leave inmates in jail for longer than necessary.

Richard Lamb and Robert W. Grant conducted a similar study of 101 women that are imprisoned in the Los Angeles County Jail system. In this study, they concluded that 70% of them had traumatizing experiences of physical violence, 40% of these women were involved in prostitution, and 84% of the women with children were incapable of taking care of them.

In addition, there were more mentally ill men in jail than there were women. In a study of male inmates, there appeared to have been issues of the "criminalization" of those whom were mentally ill.

An issue that resides in these studies is that there is uncertainty when trying to determine if these prisoners receive any beneficial treatment. In response to this issue, Dr. Terry Kupers mentions that when considering the large proportion of prisoners with significant mental illness, few of these Los Angeles County Jail inmates receive adequate mental health treatment.

However, mental illnesses have been and are currently being studied in the Los Angeles County Jail. For instance, several researchers studied Bipolar I disorder, and found that a way to decrease the number of inmates with Bipolar 1 disorder is by having them participate in longer psychiatric hospital stays.

One solution to this issue could be opt-out screening and vaccinations for STI's and other infectious diseases, which has the potential to improve health conditions in jail and in surrounding communities.

This can be accomplished by providing health care that many inmates, especially impoverished Blacks and Latinos, would not receive otherwise. In addition, the implementation of this action would decrease the spreading of diseases from the jail to home communities.

Using opt-out screenings and vaccinations can be used as a mechanism to reach out to inner city community health issues as well as provide a new area for research in the effectiveness in vaccinations and screenings.

While health has been one of the primary concerns within the Los Angeles County Jail, the Los Angeles County Jail system also has a bad reputation of targeting minorities for its prisons. Victor Rios argues that a new era of mass incarceration has resulted in the development of a youth control complex.

This complex resulted from a network of racialized criminalization, and the punishment arrived from institutions of authority that patrolled and incapacitated Black and Latino youth. Rios concludes that it's not policing but the harsh policing of inner cities that marks young people from their early years, effectively stigmatizing them through negative credentials before they have an opportunity to acquire the more positive forms demanded for participation in mainstream society.

Achievements

The LASD has gained an international reputation for its efforts in developing and integrating the latest law enforcement technologies, especially nonlethal weapons. Because many developers, especially those developing technologies for the U.S. Department of Defense, have little idea of the needs of domestic law enforcement.

The LASD provides experts to assist in the development and implementation of technologies that will be of service to law enforcement when fully mature.

In the late 1990s, the LASD successfully implemented a county-wide sound recorder/meter system, Shot-Stopper, to detect loud noises.

When dispatch has a call from a citizen reporting possible gunfire near their residence, these sound towers can pinpoint within about 25 to 30 feet (9.1 m) where the shots were coming from and record the sound for investigative purposes, and at the same time, relay the 'GPS' info to HQ and deputies on the street.

The system has been up and running for several years and has been responsible for numerous felony arrests.

Currently, the LASD is working with the FAA and local government officials to deploy their remote control aerial *surveillance* drone system. This would allow the Sheriff's Department to have real time imagery from the streets of Los Angeles to combat street violence and record crimes in progress, not to mention searching for missing hikers, "patrolling" behind the surf zones of the beaches and looking for lost children.

The drones are not intended to replace police helicopters, but in specific incidents could be better, cheaper and quieter to use.

Starting in 2009, LASD began leasing electric-powered Mini Cooper cars for $10 a month each. In exchange, Mini Cooper's parent company, BMW, requested feedback about the cars. One of the cars is currently being used at the Sheriff Substation at Universal City.

The LASD hired the first female deputy sheriff in the United States in 1912. Margaret Q. Adams remained a deputy in the evidence department at the Los Angeles Courthouse for 35 years, until her retirement in 1947.

Special Weapons Teams

The Special Enforcement Bureau (SEB) is the LASD's equivalent of a SWAT team, which was originally a creation of the nearby Los Angeles Police Department during the 1960s. Law enforcement agencies from across the nation and around the world often look to the LASD SEB and LAPD **SWAT** teams for training and advice, often sending experienced officers to train under both departments.

In 1992, after the riots in Los Angeles, both the LAPD SWAT and LASD SEB teams decided to work on tactics that would rescue people from dangerous crowds, and at the same time provide a way to eliminate a threat, such as a gunman, without being noticed by a hostile crowd.

In the first example, the idea was to have SWAT ride in one of the city's Air Rescue helicopter units with LAFD and LASD paramedics to enter a scene, using **SWAT** as a threat to ground opposition while LAFD paramedics could safely drop in and pick up an injured person.

In the second example, sharpshooters could be used at high altitudes in LASD air units to look for any potential threats on the ground, and at the same time neutralize any would-be killers.

Air Rescue Program

The LASD Air Rescue program is used for many emergencies in L.A. County, most notably the wildfire-prone Angeles National Forest. Persons trapped in inaccessible areas are usually found and rescued by LASD Air Rescue. The LASD has multiple Sea King helicopters for this program.

Towards the middle of 2012, LASD's Air Rescue 5 began replacing Sikorsky H-3 Sea Kings with 3 Eurocopter AS332 Super Pumas as primary rescue helicopters.

In addition to having a fleet of three Sikorsky Sea Kings, the LASD also utilizes 14 Eurocopter AS-350 AStar helicopters and 3 Hughes/Schweizer 300 series S-300C helicopters.

The Sky Knight Helicopter Program is an airborne law enforcement program in Lakewood, California which began in 1966. The unit operates using non-sworn pilots, employed by the city of

Lakewood, partnered with a sworn deputy sheriff from the Los Angeles County Sheriff's Department, Lakewood station.

The unit currently operates three Schweizer 300C helicopters, based at Long Beach airport and flies about 1,800 hours per year. Today, the Sky Knight program is completely integrated within the sheriff's tactical operations.

Five other cities (Artesia, Bellflower, Hawaiian Gardens, Paramount and Cerritos) contract with Lakewood to participate in the Sky Knight program. These five cities also contract with the Los Angeles County Sheriff's Department for police services.

Contract Law Enforcement

Cities

The LASD has entered into contracts with the numerous cities to serve as their police department/law enforcement agency. Forty-two (42) of the eighty-eight (88) cities in Los Angeles County contract with the Sheriff's Department for their complete municipal law enforcement services.

Some of the newer contract cities like Santa Clarita and West Hollywood have never had police departments. When their city governments were founded, they took over what was formerly unincorporated land, and then contracted their police responsibilities to the county sheriff. Since the department had substations in those areas, the result was to maintain the status quo.

In contrast, Compton, California, once had a police department. In 2000, the city council voted to dismantle the troubled police department and contract for police services. Compton has been at times notorious for gang violence, especially during its recent history.

Other Agencies

LASD provides dispatch services by contract to the California Department of Corrections for state parole officers. The services are provided by LASD County Services Bureau dispatchers.

Sheriff's dispatchers at the Avalon Sheriff's Station on Catalina Island also provide dispatch services for the city of Avalon Fire Department.

By liaison via the Sheriff's Scientific Services Bureau, cybercrime detection and investigation often operates in conjunction with other agencies.

Transit Contracts

- Metrolink
- Los Angeles MTA (Metro)
- Antelope Valley Transit Authority
- Foothill Transit

Community Colleges Services Bureau (#87)

- Los Angeles Community College District
- Antelope Valley College

Court Services Division

- Prisoner Transport Services with 31 of the 58 counties in California.
- Los Angeles County Marshal/Municipal Courts (Merged into LASD Court Services January 1. 1994)

Contract Custody Services

- California Department of Corrections (Housing Parole Violators)

Reserve Program

The Los Angeles County Sheriff's Department supplements its full-time ranks with over 800 reserve deputies. Reserve deputies are often civic minded people that have other full-time jobs outside of law enforcement. However some reserves may be retired peace officers, and/or former full-time officers.

CHAPTER SIX

LASD Alex Villanueva, Sheriff, LAPD Michael Moore, Police Chief, and our man, Charlie the famous PI, were driving on the 10 (Santa Monica) Freeway, as it intersects with the log-jam 110 (Harbor Freeway) near downtown Los Angeles.

They were riding in Charlie's new BMW, which he likes to call Black beauty III, because he has had three of this particular model 750IL, and they were all beautiful black in color.

Located on that intersection of the 10 and the ll0, is an absolutely wonderful hospital that is 'near and dear' to our man Charlie. You might say he owes his life to that great place.

California Medical Center is over one-hundred-years old and it is one of the finest health care facilities in Los Angeles. The doctors, nurses and staff are also some of the best in the health care industry.

Charlie was born at that outstanding hospital back in the day, however, he never tells anybody in what year that huge event took place, even if they press him about it.

Alex said to Charlie, "Hey, my amigo, let's turn on your car stereo and listen to some tunes. I think that my compadre here, Chief Moore, likes the blues just like I do, and I recall you telling me that you love 'John Lee Hooker,' the great blues master."

Michael leaned over and turned the volume up loud, real loud and at the same time opened up Charlie's cool sun-roof so that everyone in downtown LA could hear the great Blues music along with them.

Then Alex said to Michael, "If we get pulled over for loud music, by the LAPD, can you flash your badge so that our friend Charlie does not get a ticket?" The Chief laughed really loud and then responded, 10-4 Sheriff."

And Charlie yelled to Alex, louder Sheriff, turn it up louder, let the *gang bangers* know that the new L.A. Sheriff and the new L.A. Police Chief are in town."

The Boom, Boom Blues Song for the ages:

"Boom, boom (boom, boom)
I'm gonna shoot you right down
Right off your feet
Take you home with me
Put you in my house
Boom, boom, boom, boom
Mmmm, Mmmm!

I love to see you walk
Up and down the floor
When you talking to me
That baby talk,
I like it like that
You talk like that
You knock me dead
Right off my feet

A haw, haw, haw, haw
Whoa!

Once you walk that walk
And talk that talk
And whisper in my ear
Tell me that you love me
I love that talk
That baby talk,
You knock me dead
Right off my feet
A haw, haw, haw, haw
Yeah, yeah!

Walk that walk baby
Talk that talk right now baby
You can talk that talk, baby
Talk that talk, that baby talk!

Can't take it like that
No baby, I just can't!"

Alex then told Charlie and Michael that this terrific and quite famous Blues song was originally written by the late and great, 'John Lee Hooker,' produced by Vee-Jay Records, Chicago, IL, May 1, 1962.

And also, he added that a lot of very famous musicians have *'covered'* it over the years. Including but not limited to the following:

1. The fabulous, Buddy Guy

2. Muddy Waters (One of the best Bluesmen ever)

3. The Outthere Brothers

4. Yardbirds
5. Vengaboys
6. Linda Yan
7. Slick 50
8.Bruno
9. Dynamite Blues Band
10. Stevie V (From the Philippines)
11. Full Fat
12. Wayne Cochran
13. Rufus Thomas

L.A. Bank Robbery Suspects

Charlie called Peggy and Ron Edwards, Jan Smoker, and LT. Yvette Marie, and asked them who were the prime 'person (s) of interest' in the terrifying and accelerating Los Angeles (the bank robbery capital of the world) robberies?

This is the list that they came up with, and told Charlie that this was just a preliminary list, and that there very well might be several more criminal organizations and or individuals to be added at a later date.

1. The Russians:
Vicktor Karchenco (aka the *Fisherman*)
Alexandar (Alex) Kopiyka
Boris Omsk 'Big' Tvershaya

Oleg Geogi Kalmanovich
Nikoli Mironov Syeryozha
Valadimir Yelchin 'Val' Alexievich

All of these despicable, and murderous individuals, were ex-**FSB** (formerly the hated and greatly feared- KGB) officers. They stole a lot of money, gold and silver, and a ton of weapons when they left their former 'handlers.'

2. The Deadly Hong Kong Triad:
Formerly known as the "White Lotus Family" (San Ho Hui). And thought to be over 250 years old!
Xi Keqiang
Sun Yee On
Li Dejiang
Zhang Zhengsheng

3. The North Korean Criminal Organization:
Known as "Kkangpae Communist Society".

Also, they are said to be part of the North Korean Mafia, and the Japanese Yakuza.

This highly successful criminal enterprise is well known to Interpol, as very sophisticated Identity theft experts, blackmail, and holding-ransom of computer access of USA and European, hospitals, banks, and even government agencies.

And are also responsible for bank and high-end jewelry store robberies all around the world, especially in the United States and the UK.

Pak Pong Ju, who was called the 'Supreme Leader'

Chung Jong-Un
Choe Il-Sung
Pong Tu-bong
Ryong Rae Yong-gon
And

Charlie told LT. Yvette Marie, that he really liked Korean (South Korean) people. They have a great, honorable and very ancient culture, are very polite, and very respectful. They are also highly intelligent people and their children love to learn and excel at school.

Then Yvette said to Charlie, "My favorite Jefe ever, I love Korean people just like you do. And also, I love and I know you do too, the Korean people in the North. They are treated so inhumanely and terribly, and yet they endure and they survive."

Then she added, "I pray for the good people in the north to be free one day, and one day very soon." Charlie quickly replied, "Yvette, my wonderful daughter, you are so kind and thoughtful to say that, and yes, I defiantly agree with you 100%."

4. The world roving Romanian Gypsyies:
Known all over the world by the name, "The Emil Matasareanu gang."

Klaus Lohannis, was just simply known as the 'Boss'
Ludovic Orban
Titus Corlajean
Marcel Ciolacu

Just as Charlie's terrific A-Team and Yvette and Peggy stated to El Jefe before, this is just a preliminary list of potential culprits and possible guilty parties. They assured Charlie and Sarge, that they are still working, working really hard, to 'vet' these criminals as well as to develop new and additional robbery suspects.

CHAPTER SEVEN

The Chief of Police of one of the finest Police Departments in Orange County, albeit, not the largest, John Burks, told Charlie, Sarge and LT Yvette Marie, when he was asked by them, the brief history of the Brea PD.

Brea Police Department

Several people in the Orange County Law Enforcement community, as well as many citizens, believe that Chief Burks is one of the finest police chief's that the great city of Brea, has ever had.

Command Staff

The Brea Police Department is divided into the Uniform and Investigative Divisions, directed by two captains. Read on to meet Captain Hayden and Captain Hawley.

Communications

Communications, also known as the 911 Dispatch Center, is the first point of contact with the department when citizens are in need of police service.

Core Values

We take our commitment to the community and the police department very seriously. It isn't just a job to us.

Crime Suppression Unit

The Crime Suppression Unit (CSU) is designed to identify current and emerging crime trends.

Department History

Going back nearly to the early 20th century, the Brea Police Department has a rich tradition of community service. In fact, the history of the law enforcement in Brea goes back to a time even before the city was incorporated in 1917.

In Memoriam

We respectfully remember those who have served our communities and died in the' line of duty'.

Investigative Services Division

Police officers assigned as detectives work in one of several investigation units focusing on specialized case work.

K-9 Unit

The Canine (K-9) unit is a valuable tool used to locate and apprehend suspects, prevent officer and suspect confrontations, and to identify and retrieve narcotics-related assets.

Patrol Division

The patrol officers that work in the Patrol Division of the police department and are often called first responders.

Professional Standards Unit

We respect the community we serve. We hold our officers to the highest standards.

S.W.A.T. Unit

The Special Weapons and Tactics team is a designated unit of law enforcement officers that is specifically trained and equipped to work as a coordinated team responding to critical incidents.

Threat Management Unit

The Brea Police Department Threat Management Unit (TMU) was created to head off potentiallyserious problems before they start.

Traffic Unit

The goal of the Traffic Unit is to ensure traffic safety. These motor (motorcycle) officers receive specialized training in order to focus their efforts on preventing problems and enforcing traffic safety laws.

Command Staff

UNIFORM DIVISION COMMANDER

Captainin Gregg Hayden is the Uniform Division commander and is a 27-year veteran of the Brea Police Department. Captain Hayden has held many different positions throughout his career including assignments as both a detective and an investigation supervisor.

He holds both Bachelor and Master's degrees from Cal State Fullerton and Chapman University, respectively. Captain Hayden provides oversight for all investigative efforts such as the Detective Bureau and the Crime Suppression Unit.

Members of the Investigative Division also include Crime Scene Investigation, Property & Evidence, Crime Analysis, and the Records staff.

INVESTIGATION DIVISION COMMANDER

Captain Adam Hawley is a 20-year veteran of the Brea Police Department. Before being sworn-in as a Police Officer, he served as a Brea Police Cadet for four years while attending university. During his career, Captain Hawley worked as a Patrol Officer, Mall Liaison Officer, Field Training Officer, Property Crimes Detective, Sex Crimes Detective, FBI Internet Crimes Against Children Task Force Officer, Patrol Sergeant, Detective Sergeant, Patrol Lieutenant/East Area Commander, and Professional Standards Lieutenant.

Captain Hawley holds a Master's degree from California State University Long Beach, a Bachelor's degree from California State University Fullerton, certificates in Leadership and Human Resources from California State University Fullerton, is a graduate of the Sherman Block Supervisory Leadership Institute Class #354, and is currently attending California P.O.S.T. Command College Class #66.

EAST AREA COMMAND

Lieutenant Chris Harvey is the East Area Commander and has been an officer with the Brea Police Department since 1999 but joined the department as an Explorer in 1992. Lieutenant Harvey holds a Bachelor's degree in Kinesiology/Sports Medicine from California State University of Fullerton.

During his career with the Brea Police Department he has served as a patrol officer, detective, Corporal/Field Training Officer, patrol sergeant, detective sergeant and a founding member of the crime suppression unit. In his free time, he enjoys spending time with his wife and four kids, hiking in the north Orange County area and his favorite restaurant in Brea is D'Vine.

The East Area is the largest patrol area geographically in the city. The east command encompasses nearly all area east of the 57 freeway and includes Carbon Canyon, the Blackstone development, Wildcatters Park, the Brea Sports Park, and the large retail corridor on Imperial Highway with stores that include Walmart, Nordstrom Rack, and Albertson's Grocery.

WEST AREA COMMAND

Lieutenant Phil Rodriguez is the West Area Commander and has been with the Brea Police Department for close to 23 years and holds a Bachelor's degree in Psychology from Vanguard University. He enjoys traveling and loves to watch and support his daughters play basketball and volleyball.

Lieutenant Rodriguez is well-known throughout the community as one of the co-hosts of Brea 411, the department's weekly Facebook Live. His favorite Brea restaurant is The Cheesecake Factory.

The West Area Command encompasses both residential and commercial properties. The boundaries include Brea Boulevard to the east, Imperial Highway to the south, and the city limits to the north and west.

CENTRAL AREA COMMAND

Captain David Alan Dickinson is the Central Area Commander and is a 28-year veteran of the Brea Police Department. Captain Dickinson holds a Master's Degree in Management and Leadership from Webster University; and a Bachelor's degree from California

State University of Fullerton, in Criminal Justice (with a minor in Geography-City Development).

In his free time, he enjoys running several miles a day, and trying different restaurants with his lovely wife, Desiree, and his marvelous and very creative daughter, Morgan Marie. Some of their favorite Brea restaurants are Cha Cha's Latin Kitchen, the Olive Pit Grill and Alza Osteria.

The Central Area Command is defined geographically by the 57 freeway to the east, Downtown Brea to the west, Imperial Highway to the south, and the Rails to Trails to the north. This area includes much of our central retail core including the Brea Mall and Downtown Brea.

Captain Dickinson has just recently received his Ph.D. in Education at night school. Therefore, he is now Doctor David Alan Dickinson. He is the only member of the Dickinson family to ever become a Doctor. Also, he is planning on, when he retires from the great Brea PD, teaching at Cal State University-Fullerton in the Criminal Justice and Business Management Departments.

And in addition, it is said that he is be one of the brightest, and bravest, law enforcement officers in all of Orange County, California.

SOUTH AREA COMMAND

Lieutenant Kelly Carpenter is the South Area Commander and has been with the Brea Police Department for 28 years. Lieutenant Carpenter holds a Master's degree in Management, a Bachelor's degree in Criminal Justice and an executive certificate in counter terrorism.

He is also certified as a Terrorism and Homeland Security Specialist by the Governor's Office of Emergency Services. His hobbies include traveling, hiking and his favorite restaurant in Brea is Ichiban.

The South Area includes both residential and business/retail centers. This command area includes all areas south of Imperial Highway and east to the 57 freeway. The area also includes areas west of Brea Boulevard (except Downtown Brea) and south of Lambert to the western city boundary.

CHAPTER EIGHT

Charlie said to OCSD LT. Yvette Marie, “Mi’ja, wonderful daughter of mine, do you remember the very popular hit song by Randy Newman, ‘I Love L. A’?” Yvette immediately replied, “Si my great Pappy, I remember it well, me and all of my friends in school, went around singing it all of the time, back in the day.”

Charlie said let’s play it on my iPod just for the fun of it, get Sarge on your cell phone speaker so he can sing along with the two of us, alright?” She laughed and then laughed some more. *She has such a marvelous laugh*, Charlie thought.

Yvette started to laugh, again, and Charlie asked her what was so funny? She responded, “My Jefe, do you know how bad my beloved husband’s voice is? I love him dearly, as you know, but he really cannot sing very well.”

Charlie then joined her in a lot of laughter, at Sarge’s expense of course, and he said to Yvette, “My girl, yes I have heard Sarge sing before, and you are correct, his is pretty bad, but let’s play along and tell him that he sounded great, he will never know the difference anyway, OK?”

Then Yvette started to cry, with laughter, and finally asked Charlie, her adopted dad, “How could anyone sing that badly?” And Charlie smiled big, and said, “I think he took lessons on how to sing poorly, and that is how he got so good at singing so bad.”

Yvette was still crying and laughing all at the same time, and composed herself and called Sarge on her speed dial on her new 'gold' iPhone.

{This song was Inspired by the great, and extremely talented, 'Randy Newman' and adapted for this said novella by Charles Warner Kennedy 'Charlie' O'Brien}.

I Love L. A.

"I hate New York City, and Jersey too
It's cold and it's damp
And all the people dress like stock brokers
Let's leave Chicago to the Eskimos
The southside is a little too rough
For you and me, my pretty valley girl!

Rollin' down the Imperial Highway
In my 1964 Chevy Impala low-rider with a big 409
With a big sexy redhead at my side
Santa Ana winds blowin' hot from the north
And we, we, was born to ride!

Roll down the window, put down the convertible top
Crank up the Beach Boys, baby, don't ever let it stop
No, don't let that music stop
We're gonna ride it till we just can't ride it no more!

From the South Bay to the Valley
From the West Side to the East Side
Everybody's very happy, ecstatic even, you could say
'Cause the Sun is shining all of the time
Looks like another 'perfect' day in L.A.

I love L. A. (We love it)
I love L. A. (We love it)

Look at that High Sierra mountains
Look at those gigantic Redwood trees
Look at that poor soul over there, man
He's down and praying on his bending knees
Look at these L. A. women, Wow
There ain't nothin' like em, nowhere!

Century Boulevard (We love it)
Victory Boulevard (We love it)
Santa Monica Boulevard (We love it)
Sixth Street (We love it, we love it)
We just love L. A.

I love L. A. (We love it)
I love L. A. (We love it)
I love L.A. (We love it)"

Peggy Edwards, of Charlie's A-Team told Charlie that the history of the fabulous song, according to 'Randy Newman' himself, was that the original title was to be "Something to sing about".

While on a jet plane with the incomparable Eagles drummer, Don Henley, Don told Randy he should write a song about his beloved L.A. Then, Don told him maybe a title of 'Something to sing about' might, just might, work out well for him.

And boy was Don right, it was one of Randy's best-selling songs, ever. Randy wrote many, many absolutely wonderful songs with much more complicated lyrics, however, none found the heart and mind of the Angelenos like this one did.

After some time, Randy, finally found the words, and perfect melody, for what would become a Mega Hit for him, "I love L.A." Randy always remembered that it was his good friend, Don, who gave him the idea for the song.

Inspired, and originally written by the one and only pop-rocker, 'Randy Newman,' Producer Lenny Waronker, Warner Brothers Recording company, 1983.

[New song lyrics by Charlie Warner Kennedy 'Charlie' O'Brien, April 15, 2020].

LOS ANGELES PD INFORMATION
Section I

The first specific Los Angeles police force was founded in 1853 as the Los Angeles Rangers, a volunteer force that assisted the existing L.A. County forces. The Rangers were soon succeeded by the Los Angeles City Guards, another volunteer group. Neither force was particularly efficient and Los Angeles became known for its violence, gambling and vice.

The first paid force was created in 1869, when six officers were hired to serve under City Marshal William C. Warren.[1] By 1900, under John M. Glass, there were 70 officers, one for every 1,500 people. In 1903, with the start of the Civil Service, this force was increased to 200.

The CBS radio show *'Calling All Cars'* hired LAPD radio dispatcher Jesse Rosenquist to be the voice of the dispatcher. Rosenquist was already famous because home radios could tune in to early police radio frequencies.

As the first police radio dispatcher presented to the public ear, he was the voice that actors went to when called upon for a radio dispatcher role.

During World War II, under Clemence B. Horrall, the overall number of personnel was depleted by the demands of the military. Despite efforts to maintain numbers, the police could do little to control the 1943 "Zoot Suit" Riots.

Horrall was replaced by retired United States Marine Corps General William A. Worton, who acted as interim chief until 1950, when *William H. Parker* succeeded him and would serve until his death in 1966.

Parker advocated police professionalism and autonomy from civilian administration. However, the Bloody Christmas scandal in 1951 led to calls for civilian accountability and an end to alleged police brutality.

The iconic television series **Dragnet**, with LAPD detective '**Joe Friday**' as the primary character, was the first major mass media representation of the department. Real LAPD operations inspired Jack Webb to create the series and close cooperation with department officers let him make it as realistic as possible, including authentic police equipment and sound recording on-site at the police station.

Due to *Dragnet*'s popularity, LAPD Chief Parker "became, after **J. Edgar *Hoover***, the most well-known and respected law enforcement official in the nation" at that time. In the 1960s, when the LAPD under Chief Thomas Reddin, expanded its community relations division and began efforts to reach out to the African-American community, **Dragnet** followed suit with more emphasis on internal affairs and community policing than solving crimes, the show's previous mainstay.

Under Parker, the LAPD created the first SWAT (Special Weapons and Tactics) team in U.S. law enforcement. Officer John Nelson and, then-Inspector Daryl Gates, created the program in 1965 to deal with threats from radical organizations such as the Black Panther Party operating during the Vietnam War era.

The old headquarters for the LAPD was the Parker Center, named after former chief **William H. 'Bill' Parker**, which still stands at 150 N. Los Angeles St. A new headquarters replaced it in October 2009 and is located 300 yards (270 m) west in the purpose-built Police Administration Building at 100 W. 1st St., immediately south of the Los Angeles City Hall.

Organization

Board of Police Commissioners

The 'Los Angeles Board of Police Commissioners' also known as the 'Police Commission', is a five-member body of appointed officials which oversees the LAPD. The board is responsible for setting policies for the department and overseeing the LAPD's overall management and operations. The Chief of Police reports to the board, but the rest of the department reports to the chief.

Office of the Inspector General

The Office of the Inspector General is an independent part of the LAPD that has oversight over the department's internal disciplinary process and reviewing complaints of officer misconduct. It was created by the recommendation of the Christopher Commission and it is exempt from civil service and reports directly to the Board of Police Commissioners.

The current Inspector General is Mark P. Smith who was formerly the Constitutional Policing Advisor for the Los Angeles County Sheriff's Department. The OIG receives copies of every complaint filed against members of the LAPD as well as tracking specific cases along with any resultant litigation.

The OIG also conducts audits on select investigations and conducts regular reviews of the disciplinary system in order to ensure fairness and equality. As well as overseeing the LAPD's disciplinary process, the 'Inspector General' may undertake special investigations as directed by the Board of Police Commissioners.

Office of the Chief

The Office of the Chief of Police has the responsibility for assisting the Chief of Police in the administration of the department.

Chief of Staff

The Chief of Staff is responsible for coordinating the flow of information from command staff to ensure that the Chief is fully informed prior to making decisions, performing and coordinating special administrative audits and investigations, and assisting, advising, and submitting recommendations to the Chief of Police in matters involving employee relations.

The Office of the Chief of Staff is composed of the Board of Police Commissioners Liaison, the Public Communications Group, the Media Relations Division, and the Employee Relations Group.

Office of Constitutional Policing and Policy

The Director of the Office of Constitutional Policing and Policy, currently Police Administrator III Arif Alikhan, also reports directly to the Office of the Chief. The office is divided into the Audit Division, Governmental Liaison Section, OMBUDS Section, and the Risk Management & Legal Affairs Group.

The Risk Management & Legal Affairs Group is further divided into the Risk Management and Policies Division, the Legal Affairs Division, and the Strategic Planning Section.

Professional Standards Bureau

The Professional Standards Bureau is the investigative arm of the Chief to identify and report corruption and employee behavior that discredits the LAPD or violates a department policy, procedure, or practice.

The Professional Standards Bureau is divided into the Internal Affairs Group, the Special Operations Division, and the Force Investigation Group.

Information Technology Group

The Information Technology Group is responsible for providing Information Technology services to the department.

The Information Technology Group is composed of the following subordinate units:

- Information Technology Division

- Application Development & Support Division
- Emergency Command Control Communications System (ECCCS) Division
- Innovation Management Division

Office of Operations

The New Police Administration Building opened in 2009.

The majority of the LAPD's approximately 10,000 officers are assigned within the Office of Operations, whose primary office is located in the new Police Administration Building.

Headed by an Assistant Chief, currently Assistant Chief Robert Arcos, and the Assistant to the Director, who is a Commander, the office comprises four bureaus and 21 police stations, known officially as "areas" but also commonly referred to as "divisions".

The Office of Operations also has a dedicated Homeless Coordinator reporting directly to the Assistant Chief. The Community Engagement Group also reports to the Assistant Chief.

The 21 police stations or "divisions" are grouped geographically into four command areas, each known as a "bureau". The latest areas, "Olympic" and "Topanga", were added on January 4, 2009.

Operations—Central Bureau

The Central Bureau is responsible for downtown Los Angeles and eastern Los Angeles, and is the most densely populated of the four patrol bureaus. It currently consists of five patrol divisions.

Operations—South Bureau

South Bureau oversees South Los Angeles with the exception of Inglewood and Compton, which are both separate cities that maintain their own law enforcement agencies (in Compton's case, a contract with the Los Angeles County Sheriff's Department). The South Bureau currently consists of four patrol divisions, and the South Bureau Homicide Division.

77th Street Division

77th Street Area (#12) serves a portion of South Los Angeles, roughly in an area south of Vernon Avenue, west of the Harbor Freeway, north of Manchester Avenue and points west to the city limits, including the Crenshaw region.

A section of South Central Los Angeles that borders Florence, Central and Manchester Avenues to the Harbor Freeway is also part of this division.

The division's address is 7600 S. Broadway, Los Angeles, CA 90003. The division also has a Junior Cadets program separate from the cadet program. The Junior Cadets' age range is between 9 and 13; after age 13 they can join the Cadets. The Junior Cadets program is exclusive to the 77th street division.

Harbor Division

Harbor Area (#5) serves San Pedro, Wilmington, Harbor City, and the Harbor Gateway annex south of Artesia Boulevard. This division often works with the Port of Los Angeles Police. The 260 Harbor division members operate out of a $40-million, 50,000-square-foot (4,600 m2) police station, that was opened in April 2009 on John S. Gibson Blvd.

Southeast Division

Southeast Area (#18), like the 77th Street Division, patrols a part of South Los Angeles.[38] Their area extends to the city limits north of Artesia Boulevard, and includes Watts and areas south of Manchester Avenue.

Southwest Division

Southwest Area (#3) serves all of the city limits south of the Santa Monica Freeway, west of the Harbor Freeway, north of Vernon Avenue, and east of the Culver City/Lennox/Baldwin Hills area. This section also includes the University of Southern California and Exposition Park.

Operations—Valley Bureau

The Valley Bureau is the largest of the four patrol bureaus in terms of size (about 221 square miles), and overseas operations within the San Fernando Valley. It currently consists of seven patrol divisions.

Mission Division

The Mission Area (#19) community police station began operations in May 2005. This was the first new station to be created in more than a quarter of a century. The Mission Area covers the eastern half of the old Devonshire and the western half of the Foothill Divisions in the San Fernando Valley, including Mission Hills and Panorama City.

Devonshire Division

The Devonshire Area (#17) is responsible for the northwestern parts of the San Fernando Valley, including parts of Chatsworth and Northridge.

Foothill Division

The Foothill Area (#16) patrols parts of the San Fernando Valley (including Sun Valley) and the Crescenta Valley (including Sunland-Tujunga).

North Hollywood Division

See also: North Hollywood shootout

The North Hollywood Area (#15) is responsible for Studio City, Valley Village and the North Hollywood Region.

Van Nuys Division

The Van Nuys Area (#9) serves the areas of Van Nuys, Sepulveda and Sherman Oaks.

West Valley Division

The West Valley Area (#10) is responsible for parts of the San Fernando Valley, including parts of Encino, Northridge, Reseda and Winnetka, where it is based.

Topanga Division

The Topanga (#21) community police station began operations in January 2009. It is responsible for parts of the San Fernando Valley that are within the city's 3rd Council District, including Woodland Hills and Canoga Park, where it is based.

Operations—West Bureau

The West Bureau's operations cover most of the well-known areas of Los Angeles, including Hollywood, Westwood, the Hollywood Hills area, the UCLA campus and Venice. This does not include Beverly Hills and Santa Monica, which are separate cities from Los Angeles and maintain their own law enforcement agencies. The West Bureau currently consists of five patrol divisions.

Hollywood Division

The Hollywood Area (#6) Community Police Station serves the Hollywood region, including the Hollywood Hills, Hollywood Boulevard and the Sunset Strip.

Wilshire Division

The Wilshire Area (#7) Community Police Station serves the Mid-Wilshire "Miracle Mile" region, including Koreatown, Carthay, and the Fairfax District.

Pacific Division

The Pacific Area (#14) Community Police Station serves the southern portion of West Los Angeles, including Venice Beach Venice and Playa del Rey. Some officers assigned to the Pacific Division are commonly assigned to work with the Los Angeles Airport Police at the Los Angeles International Airport. Pacific Division was formerly known as "Venice Division".

West Los Angeles Division

The West Los Angeles Area (#8) community police station serves the northern portion of the West Side. Communities within its service area include Pacific Palisades, Century City, Brentwood, Westwood, West Los Angeles and Cheviot Hills. UCLA, which also has its own police department, and Twentieth Century Fox are both located there.

Olympic Division

The Olympic (#20) community police station opened its doors on January 4, 2009, with an open house on January 17. The Olympic Area will be a small section of the Hollywood Division, and is composed of areas from Rampart and Wilshire divisions.

It provides services to a 6.2-square-mile (16 km2) area of the Mid-City region, including Koreatown and a section of the Miracle Mile, with a population of 200,000. The 54,000-square-foot (5,000 m2) station is located at the southeast corner of Vermont Avenue and Eleventh Street and houses 293 officers. The construction cost was $34 million.

Office of Special Operations

The Office of Special Operations is an office that was created in 2010 by then-Chief Charlie Beck. Headed by an Assistant Chief, currently Assistant Chief Horace Frank, the office comprises the Detective Bureau, the Counter Terrorism and Special Operations Bureau, and the Transit Services Bureau.

Detective Bureau

The Detective Bureau consists of several divisions and sections responsible for investigating a variety of crimes.

The Detective Bureau also houses the COMPSTAT (Computer Statistics) Division which maintains crime data. It holds regular weekly meetings within a purpose-built suite in the new Police Administration Building with the Chief of Police and senior officers. COMPSTAT is based on the NYPD CompStat unit that was created in 1994 by former LAPD Chief William Bratton, while he was still a NYPD Police Commissioner. He implemented the LAPD version upon becoming Chief of Police in 2002.

Structure of the Detective Bureau

Detective Services Group

- Robbery-Homicide Division (RHD)
- Homicide Special Section (HSS)
- Robbery Special Section (RSS)
- Special Assault Section (SAS)
- Cold Case Special Section (CCSS)
- Special Investigation Section (SIS)

Juvenile Division

- Gang and Narcotics Division
- Commercial Crimes Division

Detective Support and Vice Division

- Mental Evaluation Unit
- Threat Management Unit
- Forensic Science Division (FSD)
- Technical Investigation Division (TID)

COMPSTAT Division

CHAPTER NINE

LOS ANGELES PD INFORMATION
Section II

Counter Terrorism and Special Operations Bureau:
The Counter Terrorism and Special Operations Bureau provides the Los Angeles Police Department specialized tactical resources in support of operations during daily field activities, unusual occurrences and, especially, during serious disturbances and elevated terrorism threat conditions.

Counter Terrorism and Special Operations Bureau was created from the merger of the Counter Terrorism and Criminal Intelligence Bureau with the Special Operations Bureau in 2010.

Structure of the Counter Terrorism and Special Operations Bureau
Special Operations Group
Metropolitan Division
A, B, C, and G Platoons: Crime Suppression
D Platoon: Special Weapons and Tactics (SWAT)
E Platoon: Mounted Unit
H Platoon: Municipal Executives Protection Detail
K-9 Platoon: Canine Unit
M Platoon: Administrative and Operations Planning
Air Support Division
Security Services Division

Counter-Terrorism Group
Major Crimes Division
Emergency Services Division

Transit Services Bureau

The Transit Services Bureau supervises the Transit Services Group, responsible for providing security and law enforcement to all of the bus and rail lines within the city of Los Angeles, and the Traffic Group, responsible for overseeing the four Geographical Traffic Divisions which handles traffic-related duties, such as accident investigation and the issuing of citations/tickets.

Traffic Divisions also conduct DUI enforcement through a DUI Task Force composed mostly of motorcycle or "motor" officers. In addition to this overt enforcement activity, the traffic detective bureau houses a Habitual Traffic Offender Unit (also known as an H2O detail), which conducts undercover surveillance of habitual DUI offenders and other criminals with suspended driver's licenses.

Structure of the Transit Services Bureau

Transit Services Group

Transit Services Division

Traffic Group
Central Traffic Division
South Traffic Division
Valley Traffic Division
West Traffic Division

Office of Support Services

The Office of Support Services oversees the department's communications services and matters related to personnel and training, LAPD facilities, vehicles, and fiscal operations.

The Office of Support Services is headed by an Assistant Chief, currently Assistant Chief Beatrice Girmala, the office is divided into the Critical Incident Review Division, Behavioral Science Services, Fiscal Operations Division, Administrative Services Bureau, and the Personnel and Training Bureau.

The Office of Support Services has existed in the LAPD under multiple names, first as the Office of Support Services under Chief William Bratton, then as the Office of Administrative Services, under Chief Charlie Beck, and now once again, as the Office of Support Services under Chief Michel Moore. Even though the office has undergone multiple name changes, its primary mission has always stayed the same.

Administrative Services Bureau

Support Services Group
Communications Division
Custody Services Division
Motor Transport Division
Records and Identification Division
Property Division
Facilities Management Division

The Communications Division also houses the Department Operations Center (DOC), formerly known as RACR or Real-Time Analysis and Critical Response Division which began operations in March

2006. The RACR/DOC is composed of the Department Operations Section, which includes the Department Operations Center Unit, Department Operations Support Unit and the Incident Command Post Unit; Detective Support Section and the Crime Analysis Section.

Personnel and Training Bureau
Training Group
Training Division
In-Service Training Division
Police Training & Education Director
Personnel Group
Personnel Division
Recruitment and Employment Division
Employee Assistance Unit
Officer Representation Section
Rank structure and insignia

Position	*Description*
Staff Officer	Any rank above Captain
Commanding Officer	Any Officer in charge of a Bureau
Director	Any Officer commanding an Office
Incident Commander	Any Officer who takes command in an emergency
Watch Commander	Any Officer in charge of a specific watch
Supervisor	Any Officer engaged in field supervision

Officer in Charge — Any Officer in charge of a Section

Specialized unit insignia are worn at the top of the sleeve beneath the shoulder for officers assigned to the traffic divisions, and Air Support Division. Officers assigned to Area Patrol Divisions have historically not worn any departmental shoulder patch on their uniforms.

Service stripes are worn above the left cuff on a long-sleeved shirt. Each silver stripe represents five years of service in the LAPD.

Supervisory Terminology

The following names are used to describe supervision levels within the LAPD:

As detectives are considered specialists within the LAPD, they are normally considered to be separate from the uniformed line of command. The senior-most detective is therefore permitted to take charge of an incident when it is necessary for investigative purposes, superseding the chain-of-command of other higher-ranking officers in attendance.

Chiefs of Police

Los Angeles Police Department Chiefs of Police

Since 1876, there have been 57 appointed chiefs of the Los Angeles Police Department. William Parker was the longest serving police chief in the Los Angeles Police Department history, serving for 16 years as the chief of the LAPD.

Staffing Limitations

The Los Angeles Police Department has suffered from chronic underfunding and under-staffing in recent years. Compared to most other major cities in the United States, and though it is the third-largest police department in the country, Los Angeles has historically had one of the lowest ratios of police personnel to population served.

Former police chief William J. Bratton made enlarging the department one of his top priorities (Bratton has been quoted as saying, "You give me 4,000 more officers and I'll give you the safest city in the world").

Los Angeles has one police officer for every 426 residents. As a point of comparison, New York City has one police officer for every 228 residents. For Los Angeles to have the same ratio of officers to residents as New York City, the LAPD would need to have nearly 17,000 officers.

Further points of comparison include Chicago, which has a ratio of one officer per 216 citizens and Philadelphia, whose officer per citizen ratio is 1 to 219.

In recent years, the department had been conducting a massive recruiting effort, with a goal of hiring an additional 1,500 police officers.

The city has three specialized agencies, not affiliated with the LAPD directly, which serve the Port, the Airport, and the Unified School District.

Art Theft Detail

The LAPD's Art Theft Detail "is the only full-time municipal law enforcement unit in the United States devoted to the investigation of art crimes." The longtime head and often sole member of the unit, is Detective Don Hrycyk, who in 2014 was described as being a 40-year veteran of the department with twenty years as the only known full-time art detective in the United States.

According to the LAPD, the unit has recovered over $121 million in stolen works since 1993. The Art Theft Detail is part of the Burglary Special Section of the Detective Bureau of the LAPD.

Union

The Los Angeles Police Protective League (LAPPL) is the labor union for LAPD officers up to the rank of lieutenant. It is one of the finest and most proactive police officer unions in the nation, according to Charlie.

Cadet Program

Los Angeles Police Department Cadet Program

The LAPD has its own version of the police explorer programs that are present in many police departments called the Cadet Program. The program was formerly called the explorer program but it was changed to the Cadet Program after the police commission broke off their partnership with the Boy Scouts over their rules policy of barring gays, atheists and agnostics from being troop leaders.

In order to join the cadet program a person must be between the ages of 13 and 21, meet certain academic requirements, have no serious criminal record, meet several other requirements, and complete the Cadet Academy.

The newer Cadet Program shifted focus from the old Explorer Program, which tried to guide members to a career in law enforcement, to a program that tries to give cadets a solid foundation in life and to help them prepare for whatever careers they choose, by offering things like tutoring and college scholarships, to different cadets in need of assistance.

The cadets complete courses, not only on law enforcement but also on citizenship, leadership, financial literacy and other different skill sets. Cadets work different positions including 'ride-a-long's,' crowd control, charity assistance, working in stations, and other tasks.

The cadet program has posts at all of the LAPD's regional divisions as well as specialized divisions, including the Metropolitan Division and the communications division and as of 2014 there were 5,000 cadets.

Demographics

Up to the Gates administration, the LAPD was predominantly white (80% in 1980), and many officers had resided outside the city limits. Simi Valley, the Ventura County suburb that later became infamous as the site of the state trial that immediately preceded the 1992 Los Angeles riots, has long been home to a large concentration of LAPD officers, most of them white. A 1994 ACLU study of officers' home zip codes, concluded that over 80% of police officers resided outside the city limits.

Hiring quotas began to change this during the 1980s, but it was not until the Christopher Commission reforms that substantial numbers of black, Hispanic, and Asian officers began to be hired onto the force.

Minority officers can be found in both rank-and-file and leadership positions in virtually all divisions, and the LAPD is starting to reflect the general population.

The LAPD was, in 1910 to hire the first female police officer in the United States, Alice Stebbins Wells. On the LAPD, through the early 1970s, women were classified as "policewomen".

Through the 1950's, their duties generally consisted as working as matrons in the jail system, or dealing with troubled youths working in detective assignments. Rarely did they work any type of field assignment and they were not allowed to promote above the rank of sergeant.

A lawsuit by a policewoman, Fanchon Blake, from the 1980's instituted court ordered mandates that the department begin actively hiring and promoting women police officers in its ranks.

The department eliminated the rank of "Policeman" from new hires at that time along with the rank of "Policewoman". Anyone already in those positions was grandfathered in, but new hires were classified instead as "Police Officers", which continues to this day. In 2002, women made up 18.9% of the force.

In 1886, the department hired its first two black officers, Robert William Stewart and Roy Green. The LAPD was one of the first two police departments in the country to hire an African-American woman officer, Georgia Ann Robinson in 1919.

Despite this, the department was slow at integration. During the 1965 Watts riots, only 5 of the 205 police assigned to South Central Los Angeles were black, despite the fact that it was the largest black community in Los Angeles.

Los Angeles' first black mayor Tom Bradley was an ex-police officer and quit the department after being unable to advance past the rank of lieutenant like other black police officers in the department.

When Bradley was elected mayor in 1972, only 5% of LAPD officers were black and there was only one black captain in the department, Homer Broome.

Broome would break down racial barriers on the force going on to become first black officer to obtain the rank of commander and the first black to command a police station--the Southwest Division which included the historically black neighborhoods of South-Central Los Angeles in 1975.

As of 2019, the Los Angeles Police Department had 10,008 officers sworn in. Of these, 81% (8,158) were male and 19% (1,850) female. The racial/ethnic breakdown:

48.8% or 4,882 was Hispanic/Latino (of any race)
30.9% or 3,090 was non-Hispanic White
9.62% or 962 was African American
7.66% or 766 was Asian
2.46 % or 246 was Filipino American

remaining were Indian and other ethnicities.

Languages

The LAPD has grown over the years in the number of officers who speak languages in addition to English. There were 483 bilingual or multilingual officers in 1974, and 1,560 in 1998, and 2,500 in 2001 that spoke at least one of 32 languages.

In 2001, a study was released that found that non-English-speaking callers to the 911 and non-emergency response lines often receive no language translation, often receive incomplete information, and sometimes receive rude responses from police employees.

The issue of a lack of multilingual officers led to reforms including bonuses and salary increases for officers who are certified in second languages.

Currently, over a third of LAPD officers are certified in speaking one or more languages other than English. The department also uses a device called the phrase-lator to translate and broadcast thousands of prerecorded phrases in a multitude of languages and is commonly used to broadcast messages in different languages from police vehicles.

Work Environment and Pay:

LAPD patrol officers have a three-day 12-hour and four-day 10-hour work week schedule. The department has over 250 types of job assignments, and each officer is eligible for such assignments after two years on patrol. LAPD patrol officers almost always work with a partner.

Unlike most suburban departments surrounding the City of Los Angeles, which deploy officers in one-officer units in order to maximize police presence and to allow a smaller number of officers to patrol a larger area.

The department's training division has three facilities throughout the city, including Elysian Park, Ahmanson Recruit Training Center (Westchester), and the Edward Davis Training Center (Granada Hills).

From spring 2007 through the spring of 2009, new recruits could earn money through sign- on bonuses ranging from $5,000 to $10,000. Those bonuses ended in 2009.

Sign-on bonuses were paid 1/2 after graduation from the academy, and 1/2 after completion of probation.

Also, $2,000 could be added for sign ons from outside the Los Angeles area for housing arrangements. As of July 2009, new recruits earned starting salaries of $56,522–61,095 depending on education level, and began earning their full salary on their first day of academy training.

In January 2010, the starting base salary for incoming police officers was lowered by 20%. At the time If the applicant had graduated from high school their starting salary would be $45,226, if they had at least 60 college units, with an overall GPA of 2.0 or better, their salary would start at $47,043, and if the applicant had fully completed a college degree, the salary would start at $48,880.

In 2014 after negotiations between the city and the police officers' union reached an agreement on police officer pay that would give pay increases to nearly 1,000 officers who joined the department since the salaries for incoming officers were cut.

The agreement also raised starting salaries for officers to $57,420, with an additional increase to $60,552 after 6 months, which would become effective in the beginning of 2015.

The agreement would also change the current overtime-payment system from a deferred payment system, which was implemented to cut costs, to a pay-as-you-go overtime system as well as increasing the overtime budget from $30 million to $70 million.

Body Cameras

Beginning in September 2013, the LAPD started a trial program for the use of body- worn cameras with 30 officers in the Skid Row area. Reports from the trial program indicated that the cameras functioned well and that they assisted in deescalating situations, although there were some technical issues with the cameras, along with slight issues with the cameras falling off of officers during movement.

In November 2014, in a sign of body-camera purchases to come, the department chose Taser International as the vendor for body cameras to be used by the LAPD after their use in the trial program earlier in the year.

On December 16, 2014, **Mayor Eric Garcetti** announced that the city would purchase 7,000 body- worn cameras from Taser for use by the department.

Patrol officers will be equipped with the cameras which will be purchased in the next fiscal year in order to outfit all patrol officers by the expected completion date in June 2016, 700 of the cameras will first be deployed to patrol officers in the Central, Mission and Newton patrol areas of the city beginning in January 2015.

$1.55 million was raised from private donors to start the body-camera program for the initial rollout phase in order to ease budget constraints for the city with another $1 million coming from the National Institute of Justice, a branch of the Department of Justice.

In total, the body cameras will most likely cost less than $10 million and will be included in Garcetti's proposed fiscal year 2019 budget. Before all of the cameras are deployed to patrol officers, the Police Commission will create a policy that governs the use of the cameras and video footage, while consulting with department and city officials, along with outside organizations, including other departments who already use body cameras.

While the commission has not created a policy yet, as of December 2014, several guidelines were already outlined by the mayor, including that officers would have to turn on the cameras whenever they arrest or detain someone for interrogation and that many public interactions, such as domestic violence interviews, would not be recorded.

The cameras may also be turned off in situations where police use deadly force. Prior to the rollout of any body- worn cameras, officers have been able to carry personally owned audio- recording devices since 1994 if they file an application and obtain the requisite permission.

CHAPTER TEN

LOS ANGELES PD INFORMAITON
Section III

Los Angeles Police Department Resources

Aviation

The LAPD Air Support Division's resources consist of 19 helicopters, ranging from 5 Bell 206 Jet Rangers to 14 Eurocopter AS350-B2's, and also a 1 Beechcraft King Air 200.

Main airship missions are flown out of downtown's Piper Tech center at the Hooper Heliport, located outside of Union Station. The LAPD also houses air units at Van Nuys Airport.

Firearms

Before the early 1970s, LAPD officers were issued the six-shot, double action/single action Smith & Wesson Model 14 .38 'Special' revolver, along with the Smith & Wesson Model 10.

From the early 1970s to 1988, officers were armed with the six-shot, double action/single action Smith & Wesson Model 15 revolver, also known as the .38 "Combat Masterpiece".

This was specifically designed at the request of the Los Angeles Police Department. It was a .38 caliber Smith & Wesson Model 10 variant with non-snag, high-profile adjustable sights.

LAPD Model 15s were often modified by an armorer to fire double-action only, meaning officers could not cock the hammer. This was to prevent accidental discharges caused by the short, light single-action trigger pull that some officers used. Many officers and detectives also carried the Model 36 "*Chief's* Special" as a backup revolver, and often off-duty.

In the patrol cars, locked to a steel bar, was an Ithaca 37, 12-gauge shotgun, loaded with "00" (double-aught) buckshot, nine pellets to the cartridge with one round in the chamber and four in the magazine tube. The shotgun was made specifically for the Los Angeles Police Department, and was called the "L.A.P.D. Special".

The shotgun was based on the Ithaca 37 "Deer slayer", which was a weapon designed to hunt large game with rifled slugs. As a consequence of being designed for use with slugs, it had rifle sights, unlike most shotguns.

The "L.A.P.D. Special" had a dull, parker-ized military finish, instead of the more usual high gloss blue finish. The barrel was 18 and a half inches long, as opposed to the twenty inches of the civilian version.

The advantages of the Ithaca Model 37 Shotgun over the Winchester, Mossberg and Remington models were that the Ithaca weighed a pound less, and could be used with equal ease by right or left-handed shooters due to the unique bottom ejection port and loading chamber it used. The Ithaca 37 has been replaced as the standard issue shotgun used by the LAPD, by the Remington 870 Police model.

In response to increasing firepower carried by criminals, including fully automatic weapons and assault rifles, LAPD patrol officers were issued the Beretta 92F. Later, officers were able to carry the Smith & Wesson Model 5906, a semi-automatic 9mm pistol, in addition to a few other approved weapons in 9mm caliber.

In response to the "North Hollywood shootout" of 1997, LAPD officers had the option of carrying the Smith & Wesson Model 4506 and 4566 service pistols in .45 ACP caliber.

Also, due to the North Hollywood incident, qualified officers were issued patrol rifles called UPR (Urban Police Rifle) consisting mainly of AR-15 variants chambered in .223 after being certified from LAPD Urban Police Rifle School.

Until 2002, LAPD officers' standard issue pistol was the Beretta 92F/92FS. However, when William Bratton was appointed Chief of the LAPD, he allowed his officers to carry the **Glock** pistol, a weapon which the two previous departments he was chief at (the New York City Police Department and the Boston Police Department) carried.

New officers graduating from the LAPD academy are now issued the Smith and Wesson M&P 9mm, and have the option of switching to Glock variants.

Officers now have the choice of carrying:

Beretta
9mm: S92F, 92FS, 8045 (4" barrel)

Smith & Wesson
9mm: M&P9, 5906, 3914, 3913, CS9, 6904, 6906

.45 ACP: 4506, 4566, 4516, 4567
.380 ACP: Smith & Wesson Bodyguard 380

Glock
9mm: Model 17, Model 19, Model 26
.40 caliber: Model 22, Model 23, Model 27
.45 ACP: Model 21, Model 30, Model 36

Along with those handguns, officers have the option of using these rifles while on duty:

Colt
5.56/.223: Colt Tactical Carbine

Smith & Wesson
5.56/.223: Smith & Wesson M&P15

The LAPD SWAT team carry the Kimber Custom TLE II in 2002, re-naming it the Kimber LAPD SWAT Custom II. Before that, LAPD SWAT carried modified Springfield or Colt M1911 pistols.

In the '80s and early '90s SWAT carried Colt RO727s and RO733s. In 2000 they began using the M4A1s. In 2010 LAPD SWAT began issuing Heckler & Koch HK416 rifles.

Currently SWAT's primary weapons are the Heckler & Koch HK416 rifle, the M4 Carbine, the FN SCAR rifle, the Colt 9mm submachine gun, the HK MP5 submachine gun, the Armalite AR-10 sniper rifle, the Remington 700 sniper rifle, the Barrett M82 sniper rifle, the M14 **sniper** rifle, the Benelli M4 Super 90 shotgun, and the Remington 870 shotgun.

The LAPD recently announced that they will be incorporating a new shotgun, the Benelli M4 Super 90, and officers will go through additional training for the use of the semi-automatic shotgun and will have to privately purchase the gun if they elect to switch from the standard pump-action Remington 870.

The LAPD also has 37mm launchers and modified "beanbag" firing Remington 870s for crowd control when less than lethal force is needed.

Awards, Commendations, Citations and Medals

The department presents a number of medals to its members for meritorious service. The medals that the LAPD awards to its officers are as follows:

BRAVERY

Medal of Valor

The LAPD Medal of Valor is the highest law enforcement medal awarded to officers by the Los Angeles Police Department. The Medal of Valor is an award for bravery, usually awarded to officers for individual acts of extraordinary heroism performed in the line of duty at extreme and life-threatening personal risk.

Liberty Award

The Liberty Award is a bravery medal for police canines killed or seriously injured in the line of duty. The award, which was inaugurated in 1990, is named after *Liberty*, a Metropolitan Division K-9 shot and killed in the line of duty. Liberty's handler received the Medal of Valor for the same incident. So far it has only been awarded once in the LAPD's history.

Police Medal for Heroism

The Police Medal is an award for bravery, usually awarded to officers for individual acts of heroism in the line of duty, though not above and beyond the call of duty, as is required for the Medal of Valor.

Police Star

The Police Star is an award for bravery, usually awarded to officers for performing with exceptional judgment and/or utilizing skillful tactics in order to defuse dangerous and stressful situations.

Police Life-Saving Medal

The Police Life-Saving Medal is an award for bravery, usually awarded to officers for taking action in order to rescue or attempt the rescue of either a fellow officer or any person from imminent danger.

Service

Police Distinguished Service Medal
Police Meritorious Service Medal
Police Meritorious Achievement Medal
Police Commission Distinguished Service Medal
Community Policing Medal
Human Relations Medal
Unit citations
Police Commission Unit Citation
Police Meritorious Unit Citation

RIBBONS

1984 Summer Olympics Ribbon

Given to any LAPD officer who saw service during the 1984 Summer Olympics from July 28 to August 12, 1984.

1987 Papal Visit Ribbon

Given to LAPD officers who were used during the September 1987 pastoral visit of Pope John Paul II.

1992 Civil Disturbance Ribbon

Given to any LAPD officer who saw service during the 1992 Los Angeles riots from April 29 to May 4, 1992.

1994 Earthquake Ribbon

Given to any LAPD officer who saw service during the 1994 Northridge earthquake from January 17 to January 18, 1994.

2000 Democratic National Convention Ribbon

Given to any LAPD officer who saw service during the 2000 Democratic National Convention from August 14 to August 17, 2000.

Reserve Service Ribbon

Awarded for 4,000 hours of service as a Reserve Police officer.

MARKSMANSHIP BADGES

The LAPD also awards Distinguished Expert, Expert, Sharpshooter, and Marksman badges to those who attain progressively higher qualification scores on its range. Bonus pay is given to qualifiers, and some assignments may require such demonstrated weapons skill beyond that earned in basic training.

FALLEN OFFICERS

Since the establishment of the Los Angeles Police Department, 210 officers have died in the line of duty. Randal Simmons was the first LAPD SWAT officer to be killed in the line of duty in 2008.

There have been two memorials to fallen LAPD officers. One was outside Parker Center, the former headquarters, which was unveiled on October 1, 1971.

The monument was a fountain made from black granite, its base inscribed with the names of the LAPD officers who died while serving the City of Los Angeles.

The old monument located at Parker Center was destroyed in the process of being transported but was replaced by a new memorial at the current police headquarters building.

This memorial, dedicated on October 14, 2009, is made up of more than 2,000 brass alloy plaques, 207 of which are inscribed with the names of fallen police officers.

Two deaths are unsolved, both of off-duty officers: Fred Early, shot in 1972, and Michael Lee Edwards, shot in May 1974.

Minor Controversies

Over the years, the Los Angeles Police Department has been the subject of a few scandals, police misconduct and other controversies, just as has any large police and/or Law Enforcement Agency.

Charlie, our PI, says that the LAPD has had fewer than any other large department in the nation. When you have thousands of officers on your force, you are bound to have a few bad apples. And as everybody knows, a few bad apples ruin the whole bunch (barrel full).

Before 1950

The widely publicized case of Christine and Walter Collins was depicted in the 2008 film *Changeling*. In March 1928, Christine

Collins reported her nine-year-old son, Walter, missing. Five months later a boy named Arthur Hutchins came forth claiming to be Walter.

When Mrs. Collins tried to tell the police that the boy was not her son, she was committed to a mental institution under a Section 12 internment. It was later determined that Walter had actually fallen victim to a child rapist/murderer in the infamous Wineville Chicken Coop Murders.

Arthur Hutchins eventually admitted that he had lied about his identity in order to get to Hollywood and meet his favorite actor, Tom Mix.

1980s

In 1986, the department purchased a 14-ton armored breaching vehicle, used to smash quickly through the walls of the houses of suspects.

The ACLU questioned the constitutionality of the vehicle. Ultimately, the California Appellate Court ruled that the vehicle was unconstitutional, violating lawful search and seizure.

Charlie was working for the LAPD back in those days, and he loved the 'Beast', he really did. He said it saved a lot of lives of brave LAPD officers.

1990s

Rampart Scandal

On 12 October 1996, LAPD Officers Rafael Pérez and Nino Durden entered the apartment of Javier Ovando. They shot the man in the back, paralyzing him from the waist down.

They then planted a gun on the unarmed man to make it appear he had attacked them. The two officers then perjured themselves.

Ovando was sentenced to 23 years in custody based on their testimony. Later one of the officers admitted his crime.

Ovando was released and in 2000 was paid $15 million for his injuries and imprisonment. The officers' actions lead to the exposure of the Rampart Scandal.

By 2001, the resulting investigations would lead to more than 75 officers being investigated or charged and over 100 criminal cases being overturned due to perjury or other forms of misconduct, much based on the plea-bargain testimony of Perez.

Charlie and LAPD Rampart Division

Charlie worked the 'Rampart Division' in the 1990s; Charlie knew both Perez and Durden and never, ever liked them. He told people that they JDSR ("Just did not smell right").

He could tell right away that they were bad cops the moment he met them, and then when he heard a lot of 'bad' stuff about them, he knew that he was right in his assumption.

Charlie has a great intuition when he meets people, he can almost, from the get go, know if they stink like a dead fish, or smell good like a 'rose' garden.

He says that is because he has a 'good' gut from people that he comes in contact with in his very dangerous line of work (e.g. being a Private Detective).

Charlie used to eat at 'Tommy's Chiliburgers', world famous burgers, dogs and fries, all buried in their secret red-hot chili sauce. It was located very close to the LAPD Rampart Division.

And most of the cops, as well as the LAFD (Los Angeles County Fire Department personnel who worked in the area, used to eat there on a very regular basis.

Of Course, the police officers and the firefighters had to share the benches with the MS-13 and local 'gang bangers' who loved Tommy's as well.

2000s
<u>2007 MacArthur Park Rallies</u>

On May Day, 2007, immigrant rights groups held rallies *in MacArthur Park* in support of undocumented immigrants.

The rallies were permitted and initially the protesters followed the terms of the permits, but some of the protesters began blocking the street. After warnings by the LAPD, the protesters failed to disperse and the rally was declared an unlawful assembly.

2010s
<u>Christopher Dorner shootings and manhunt</u>

On February 7, 2013, the LAPD was involved in what Chief Charlie Beck called, "a case of mistaken identity" when during the manhunt for the murderer and fired LAPD officer, *Christopher Dorner*, the LAPD and the Torrance Police Department fired upon pickup trucks at two separate locations, believing them to be Dorner.

The first incident took place on the 19500 Block of Redbeam Avenue. LAPD officers fired numerous shots into the back of a blue pickup truck, allegedly without warning and injured the two women inside.

The second incident, twenty-five minutes later, involved the Torrance Police shooting into the windshield of another pickup truck, narrowly missing the driver. In both cases the victims were not involved with the Dorner case.

The Dorner case itself involved allegations of impropriety by other LAPD officers, as Dorner alleged that he had been fired for reporting brutality by his training officer. The manhunt had been triggered by Dorner's alleged attacks against LAPD and ex-LAPD personnel.

In 2013, the city of Los Angeles agreed to pay the two female victims of the first incident $2.1 million each to settle the matter. The city of Torrance agreed to pay the victim of the second incident $1.8 million.

In May 2014, after much controversy in their own city, the Seattle Police Department transferred two Dragan flyer X6 UAVs to the LAPD.

The LAPD stated that the only uses for the drones would be for narrow and prescribed circumstances, such as hostage situations, but that they would not be put into use until the Board of Police Commissioners and the City Attorney crafted a policy for their use after the LA City Council ordered the policy creation.

The decision to use the drones gained significant opposition from community activists, including the ACLU and new groups founded after the announcement about drone use, including Stop LAPD Spying Coalition and the Drone-Free LAPD, No Drones, LA! activist groups who protested outside of city hall against the use of drones by the LAPD.

Charlie told Sarge that he does not like Drones, and says that they are a 'necessary evil' to use against the 'bad guys'. He is afraid, however, that they may be used against the good guys as well, on occasion.

Consent Decree

Rampart scandal

Following the Rampart Division CRASH scandal of the late 1990s and early 2000s, the United States Department of Justice entered into a consent decree with the LAPD regarding numerous civil rights violations.

Mayor *Richard J. Riordan* and the Los Angeles city council agreed to the terms of the decree on November 2, 2000. The federal judge formally entered the decree into law on June 15, 2001.

The consent decree is legally binding, and lasted until July 17, 2009, when U.S. District Court Judge Gary Feess terminated it.

Under the terms of a transitional agreement approved by Feess, the Board of Police Commissioners and the Office of Inspector

General, which monitors the department on behalf of the Board of Police Commissioners, will assume responsibility for keeping tabs on the department's efforts to fully implement a few, still-incomplete or recently finished reforms.

If lawyers for the U.S. Department of Justice are not satisfied with the oversight by the LAPD's inspector general, the agreement allows them to object and bring the department back before Feess.

The consent decree placed emphasis on several major areas, including management and supervisory measures, in order to promote civil rights integrity, along with revising critical incident procedures, documentation, investigation and review, revising the management of gang units, revising the management of confidential informants.

Program development for response to persons with mental illness, improving training, increased integrity audits, increasing the operations of the Police Commission and the Inspector General, and increasing community outreach and public information.

The consent decree includes several recommendations from the Rampart Board of Inquiry, and several consent decree provisions mandate the department to continue existing policies.

Several of the more complex, or major provisions in the decree, call for things such as the development of a risk management system, the creation of a new division to investigate all use of force now known as Force Investigative Division.

The creation of a new division to conduct audits department-wide, the creation of a field-data capture system to track the race, ethnicity or national origin of the motorists and pedestrians, stopped by the department.

The creation of an Ethics Enforcement Section within the Internal Affairs [I. A.] Group, the transfer of investigative authority to Internal Affairs of all serious personnel complaint investigations.

A nationwide study by an independent consultant on law enforcement dealing with the mentally ill to help the departments, refine its own system, a study by an independent consultant of the department's training programs, and the creation of an informant manual and database.

The Consent Decree Bureau was the LAPD bureau charged with overseeing this process. Until 2009, the commanding officer of the Consent Decree Bureau, a civilian appointed by the chief of police, was Police Administrator Gerald L. Chaleff.

CHAPTER ELEVEN

CHARLIE CALLED THE *LAPD Chief***,** Michael Moore, LASD Sheriff, Alex Villanueva, and the good Mayor of LA, Eric Garcetti, and gave them the 'Good News.' Charlie, LT. Yvette Marie, and Sarge, and the rest of the great and very *formable* A-Team, just solved the Los Angeles Bank robbery mystery.

It was not, surprisingly, the suspects that the 'band' came up with earlier in their dirty and deep-down investigation. It was not the North Koreans, not Chinese 'Triads', it was not the 'Gypsies' from Florida (or Romania), it was not even the Russians, which is what *Peggy Edwards* had believed early on.

The deadly and very frightening Los Angeles bank robbery 'crime spree,' that terrorized all of LA City and also LA County, was conducted by a *Yemeni's* terrorist crime 'Cabal'.

Charlie told the three outstanding Law Enforcement leaders, that the, 'Terrorist *Cabal'* called themselves, *"The Islamic Desert Liberation Army"* (IDLA). And their hate-filled and very prejudicial slogan was, "Death to all of the infidels and the Crusaders."

The radical Prince's 'IDLA' terrorist group, was also closely connected to another mendacious, denigrating and blood-thirsty group called "Ansar al-Sharia" also located in Yemen.

US STATE DEPARTMENT ISSUES TRAVEL WARRING

Charlie just told his A-Team that he just saw the following CNN News Release.

The United States 'Department of State' recently placed its travel warning for Yemen by including the whole country, not just the one-half that is controlled by Iranian terrorists, on its list of places it recommended Americans avoid when traveling to the extremely volatile Middle East.

The US State Department previously had warned American business people and tourists against traveling to the southern half of the country that was controlled by the Jihadist terrorists.

The whole country is now an International War Zone, despite the gallant efforts of the legitimate Yemeni's Government, with the assistance of the United States and its allies.

Kidnappings for ransom, sexual assault and battery of women tourists, robberies, and killing of all foreigners (except fellow Jihadists, of course), is sadly running rampant in this small and very poor little country.

Charlie had been to Yemen on an assignment several years ago, and he told LT. *Yvette*, that it used to be a quite beautiful country, right on the Indian Ocean. Also, he stated that the Yemeni people could not have been nicer to him.

He was there investigating fraud at the largest Yemeni bank, the 'Yemen International Deposit and Savings Bank." The President and CEO was embezzling millions of dollars of depositors' money.

And our man, Charlie, caught him with his hand in the 'till', and the Board of Directors 'cut it off.' There is no more serious crime in the Middle East than to steal, especially, someone's hard-earned life savings.

Charlie said that their Koran speaks a lot about stealing, and being dishonest with your fellow business associates and neighbors. Honesty is a very high character trait for the Muslim people.

Charlie also always says that it is the crazy terrorists, and Jihadists, that give the good Muslim believers a bad name. Lots of good clerics and Muslim religious leaders, condemn the cowardly and deplorable actions of al-Queda and ISIS, amongst many other heinous terrorist groups.

THE COUNTRY OF YEMEN

Charlie asked his great assistant and Middle East expert, *Peggy Edwards*, to do a little brief background check on the country of origin of the L. A. Bank Robbery suspects.

Peggy, fast and efficient as always, emailed the following to Charlie within 24 hours of his request to her for some background information on the country of Yemen.

With its long sea border between early civilizations, Yemen has long existed at a crossroads of cultures with a strategic location in terms of trade on the west of the *Arabian Peninsula*. Large settlements for their era existed in the mountains of northern Yemen as early as **5000 BC**.

Little is known about ancient Yemen and how exactly it transitioned from nascent *Bronze* Age civilizations to more trade-focused caravan kingdoms.

Revolution and its Aftermath

AQAP, the latter's most powerful terrorist franchise, who are likely to gain influence amid all of the pain, misery, death and chaos.

ISIL (Formerly known as ISIS) has claimed recent, bloody suicide bombings in Houthi mosques and Sana'a when it once had no known presence in the country, while AQAP has continued to seize territory in eastern Yemen *unhindered* by American drone strikes."

In February 2016 Al-Qaeda forces and *Saudi*-led coalition forces were both seen fighting *Houthi* rebels in the same battle.

In June 2019, the leader of ISIS in Yemen, Abu Osama *al-Muhajir*, was captured by the Saudi Arabian-led intervention in Yemen supported by the *United States* during a raid in the province of al-Mahra.

The operation included Yemeni 'Security Forces' and recovered a number of weapons, ammunition, computers, money in different currencies and communications equipment. Thank God It did not injure any civilians, none at all.

Brief Yemeni History

Yemen (Romanized: *al-Yaman*), sometimes spelled **Yaman**, officially the **Republic of Yemen** (Romanized: *al-Jumhūrīyah* *al-Yamanīyah*, literally "Yemeni Republic"), is a country at the southern end of the Arabian Peninsula in Western Asia.

It is the second-largest Arab sovereign state in the peninsula, occupying 527,970 square kilometers (203,850 square miles). The coastline stretches for about 2,000 kilometers (1,200 miles).

It is bordered by Saudi Arabia to the north, the Red Sea to the west, the Gulf of Aden and Guardafui Channel to the south, and Oman to the east. Yemen's territory encompasses more than 200 islands, including the Socotra islands in the *Arabian* Sea.

Yemen is a member of the Arab League, United Nations, Non-Aligned Movement and the *Organization* of Islamic Cooperation. Yemen is characterized as a failed state with high necessity of transformation.

Yemen's constitutionally stated capital is the city of *Sana'a*, but the city has been under Houthi rebel control since February 2015.

Yemen is one of the least developed countries in the world and in 2019 the United Nations reported that Yemen is the country with the most people in need of *humanitarian* aid with 24.1 million people in need.

In ancient times, Yemen was the home of the Sabaeans, a trading state that flourished for over a thousand years and included parts of modern-day Ethiopia and Eritrea. In 275 AD the region came under the rule of the later Jewish-influenced Himyarite Kingdom.

Christianity arrived in the fourth century. Islam spread quickly in the seventh century and Yemenite troops were crucial in the early

Islamic conquests. The administration of Yemen has long been notoriously difficult.

Several dynasties emerged from the ninth to 16th centuries, the Rasulid dynasty being the strongest and most prosperous. The country was divided between the Ottoman and British empires in the early twentieth century.

The Zaydi Mutawakkilite Kingdom of Yemen was established after World War I in North Yemen before the creation of the Yemen Arab Republic in 1962. South Yemen remained a British protectorate known as the Aden Protectorate until 1967 when it became an independent state and later, a *Marxist-Leninist* state.

The two Yemeni states united to form the modern Republic of Yemen (*al-Jumhūrīyah al-Yamanīyah*) in 1990. President Ali Abdullah Saleh was the first president of the new republic until his resignation in 2012. His rule has been described as a kleptocracy.

Since 2011, Yemen has been in a state of political crisis starting with street protests against poverty, unemployment, corruption, and president Saleh's plan to amend Yemen's constitution and eliminate the presidential term limit, in effect making him president for life.

President Saleh stepped down and the powers of the presidency were transferred to Vice President Abdrabbuh Mansur Hadi, who was formally elected president on 21 February 2012 in a one-candidate election.

The total absence of central government during this transition process exacerbated several clashes on-going in the country, like the armed conflict between the Houthi rebels of Ansar Allah militia and the al-Islah forces, as well as the al-Qaeda insurgency.

In September 2014, the Houthis took over Sana'a with the help of the ousted president Saleh, later declaring themselves the national government after a *coup d'état*; Saleh was shot dead by a sniper in Sana'a in December 2017.

This resulted in a new civil war and a Saudi-led military intervention aimed at restoring Hadi's government. At least 56,000 civilians and combatants have been killed in armed violence in Yemen since January 2016.

The conflict has resulted in a famine affecting 17 million people. The lack of safe drinking water, caused by depleted aquifers and the destruction of the country's water infrastructure.

It has also caused the largest, fastest-spreading **cholera** outbreak in *modern* history, with the number of suspected cases exceeding 994,751. Over 2,226 people have died since the outbreak began to spread rapidly at the end of April 2017.

Al-Qaeda

In January 2009, the Saudi Arabian and Yemeni *al-Qaeda* branches merged to form 'Al-Qaeda in the Arabian Peninsula' [AQAP], which is based in Yemen, and many of its members were Saudi nationals who had been *released* from *'Guantanamo Bay.'* Saleh released 176 al-Qaeda suspects on condition of good behavior, but terrorist activities continued.

The Yemeni army launched a fresh offensive against the Shia insurgents in 2009, assisted by Saudi forces. Tens of thousands of people were displaced by the fighting. A new ceasefire was agreed upon in February 2010.

However, by the end of the year, Yemen claimed that 3,000 soldiers had been killed in renewed fighting. The Shia rebels accused Saudi Arabia of providing support to Salafi groups to suppress Zaidism in Yemen.

On orders from U.S. President Barack Obama, U.S. warplanes fired cruise missiles at what officials in Washington claimed were Al Qaeda training camps in the provinces of Sana'a and Abyan on 17 December 2009.

Instead of hitting Al-Qaeda operatives, it hit a village, killing 55 civilians. Officials in Yemen said that the attacks claimed the lives of more than 60 civilians, 28 of them children. Another airstrike was carried out on 24 December.

The U.S. launched a series of **drone** attacks in Yemen to curb a perceived growing terror threat due to political chaos in Yemen. Since December 2009, U.S. strikes in Yemen have been carried out by the U.S. military with intelligence support from the CIA.

The drone strikes are protested by human-rights groups who say they kill innocent civilians, and that the U.S. military and CIA drone strikes lack sufficient congressional oversight, including the choice of human targets suspected of being threats to America.

Controversy over U.S. policy for drone attacks mushroomed after a September 2011 drone strike in Yemen killed Anwar al-Awlaki and Samir Khan, both U.S. citizens. Another drone strike in October 2011 killed Anwar's teenage son, Abdulrahman al-Awlaki.

In 2010, the Obama administration policy allowed targeting of people whose names are not known. The U.S. government increased military aid to $140 million in 2010. U.S. drone strikes continued after the ousting of President Saleh.

As of 2015, Shi'a Houthis are fighting against the Islamic State, Al Qaeda, and Saudi Arabia. The U.S. supports the Saudi-led military intervention in Yemen against the Houthis, but many in US SOCOM reportedly favor *Houthis*, as they have been an effective force to roll back al-Qaeda and *recently* ISIL in Yemen.

The Guardian reported that "The only groups poised to benefit from the war dragging on are the Jihadis of **Islamic State** (ISIL-ISIS) and Al-Qaeda in the Arabian Peninsula.

^^^^^

LT. *Yvette* Marie Murrieta, by working a lot of 24/7 of weeks, also discovered who the leader was and the rest of his despicable and heinous terrorist group were named:

1. ***Emir <u>Qasim</u> al-Raymi II*** was the 'head of the snake' of the Terrorist and Criminal organization. His father, a senior *Al-Qaeda leader* for many years, was killed by USA *'Navy Seals'* a few years ago, and he is trying to carry on his father's *Jihad* of Hatred, Murder and Mayhem!

Charlie told Sarge, "The Erir was a wanna-be 'Al-Qaeda' leader, however, since he could not take orders, they kicked him out of their Evil Empire several years ago, and he then started his own Terrorist Network of despots, thugs and losers."

2. ***Prince Ali Reza al-Rahman***, was the group's second in command. He was an expert with the 'blade.' He had several knives and swords made of the finest *Damascus* steel. They were all very expensive, very efficient, as well as very deadly.

He is said to have beheaded several innocent Yemeni citizens, who dared to disobey him, and also several innocent US and Collision soldiers in the middle east. The IDLA, in Yemen, have several foot soldiers kidnapping visiting tourists, journalists, and foreign government officials and hold them for ransom.

They reportedly have also 'hijacked' some foreign cargo ships and oil tankers, and have received about five million for each one that they have released. The *IDLA*, still has several ships held for ransom, and they have them stashed away in North Somalia where they have a lot of large dock (Mooring) areas, as well as a lot of security.

And the rest of their gang of 'Thieves,' and terrorists, are named as follows:

3. ***Abdul Houthi Saleh***, the 'Field Marshall.' He was the LA Bank robbery's 'get-away' driver, and he was fearless, absolutely fearless, behind the wheel. He would run red lights, run over pedestrians, and drive the wrong way on a street and/or freeway, in order to avoid the LAPD and the LASD.

He loved US made vehicles with big block V-8 HO engines, preferably 454 C.I., or higher. He picked up an old saying, while he was living and *robbing* banks in L.A, "Go Chevy V-8, or go home."

He loved that *mantra*, and he would use it all of the time, in his broken, very broken, English accent. His favorite 'get-away' vehicle was a Chevy Tahoe, jet black with *Limo* tint on all of the windows, and bullet proof tires and windows.

He would steal one from the Chevrolet Dealership in *Pasadena*, California, on the famous old Colorado Boulevard--one of the busiest car markets in Los Angeles county. He would steal a new one for each job, of course. And then 'torch' it with C-4 explosives, just as soon as the robbery went down.

4. ***Abjullah al-Iryani***, Five Star General. A former Yemeni 'War Lord' before he joined the Yemeni Army Special Forces. He was very good at Martial Arts (Karate, Tae Kwon-do and…), they trained him well.

He could shoot and kill an enemy faster than most men could draw a gun, and also, before they had a chance to blink. It is said that whenever he dispatched someone, he would smile, a big grin, because he enjoyed the 'kill' so much.

5. ***Rabbuh Akhdam al-adr***, a former Three Star General. He had been arrested three times in the past by the Yemeni Federal Government; for bank robberies, computer-fraud, computer- hacking and computer 'lock-outs' for ransom.

He supposedly had a very high I.Q. (160) and was a *'whiz kid'* with computers from when he was a young student at a very expensive boarding school in the U.K. His teachers said that he was a brilliant kid, however, he had a bad attitude and did not respect his teachers because he called them British *infidels*.

His parents owned a computer-chip manufacturing company in Yemen and were extremely wealthy, however, after he was fired from the Yemeni Army and fell in with the what he called, the wrong crowd, meaning, *"Emir and the Evil Prince,"* after that they had finally had enough and then they disowned him.

6. ***Mansur Hadrai al-Hadi***, was formerly a Two Star General. His father was very well respected in Yemen business circles and he owned and operated a very large *Caterpillar* Tractor franchise.

His father was also a General in the Yemeni Army at one time but that was before he stole enough money from the government to start his own business. He now sells heavy construction equipment to the Yemeni military, Russia and also to Iran and North Korea.

Mansur was very cunning just like a tiger and could move, and attack you, just as fast as the tiger. That is why his nickname was 'Tiger Man' and nobody wanted to mess with this 'Thailand Tiger,' no one.

7. ***Abd Ali al-Ghashmi,*** One Star General. Charlie said he was like a big bad eel, hiding in a rock formation in the Indian Ocean, just waiting to come out as you swam by, to take a nice big chunk out of you.

Eels are slippery and evil and so was he. He was very small, just like all of the other bank robbers, and fellow Yemeni's terrorists. He was only 4 foot 11 inches tall and weighed about 120 pounds.

However, every inch of him was tough, mean, and violent. He could kill you with a knife, sword (which he loved to use) and/or his bare hands. When people looked into his black and hideous eyes, they always looked away very quickly as they said that it was like looking into the eyes of the Devil, *Satan* himself.

8. ***Muhammad Rubai Nassur***, was the gang's assassin and enforcer. He had jet black eyes, just as black as his despicable heart and soul, assuming he had one. He is said to have killed his own parents, brothers and sisters, when he was only 15 years old, so that they would not be able to identify him to the authorities.

He, while extremely deadly, was said to be very charming, when he wanted to be, naturally. he was well liked by the working girls on *Hollywood* boulevard, and at the night clubs he visited, when not on a robbery look out.

He looked like a young, innocent tourist from the Middle East, and most women liked him, until he put a pillow over their faces while they slept. He was afraid to leave any witnesses who may identify him later on to the LAPD.

Yvette also found out that the criminal as well as terrorist organization, the IDLA, was affiliated with 'al-Quaeda in the Arabian Peninsula' (**AQAP**). Which is one of the most heinous terrorist groups operating in the world today.

They have committed numerous deadly attacks on United State military bases, Naval ships, and personal, in the Middle East, for years. The 'Prince' at one time was a very close friend and associate of The Demon possessed *Osama Bin Laden*, of Saudi Arabia.

The *'Prince'* as he liked to be addressed, as well as all six of his deplorable gang, were all ex-Yemeni Government 'Special Forces' members. They were all extremely well trained, always well-armed when asleep, exceptionally violent, and quite vicious men.

They were all also being sought by the 'Free Yemeni' government, a very poor and struggling Democracy, and well as the Human Rights Court in the Hague, Europe. And also, British Mi-6, the America CIA, and Interpol [in Lyon], just outside, the very romantic city of Paris, France.

Charlie has been to Paris and *the Eifel Tower*, the *Louvre* museum, *Notre Dame*, and all of the other majestic sights of the marvelous city that is quite famous, all around the globe.

He was there in 1991 when he took his son Mark, sightseeing in the UK and Europe and Spain, as a graduation present. They both had a wonderful time, and neither will ever forget how much fun they had and what indescribable artifacts that they saw.

They went with a group from his high school, students and Teachers. The kids were all great and very well behaved. And the teachers were swell too, one spoke French, another Spanish, and yet another spoke German.

Charlie also said that the French people were not very nice to the group, except the one who spoke French, they were very polite to her. Charlie heard several of the group say, "The French act like frogs and they do not like Americans at all."

Charlie has some gorgeous replicas of several Claude Monet's, Vincent Van Goughs's, and Aguste Pierre Renoir's oil on canvas, paintings hanging all over his nice well- appointed, condominium.

He says that they are worth about $30,000.00 or so, and also, he jokes that he wished he had the originals, and that they would be worth, almost one *billion* dollars!

INTERPOL (INTERNATIONAL POLICE ORGANIZATION)

Interpol *is the most interested in this criminal* and terrorist, 'Cabal.' Their full name is the 'International Police Organization,' albeit, they are never called that, just plain old Interpol. They are Located in the lovely wine county and rolling hills of the Paris (The City of Light) suburbs.

Their name *strikes* fear and trembling to all of the crooks, criminals and murderers throughout the whole wide world, it really does. They were originally founded by the UK, Germany, France and the United States.

The predecessor of Interpol started in 1914 during the First World War, then had name and charter changes in 1923, 1938, 1946, and 1956. The current elected President is Kim Jong Yang, of South Korea.

And the *Secretariat* runs the day-to-day operations of Interpol. It is headed up by General Jurgen Stock, the former head of Germany's very successful 'Federal Criminal Police.'

They have an annual budget of about 113 million Euros (approximately two hundred million USA dollars) with 800 employees who work all over the globe. In order to become an Interpol Agent, you must first have served in law enforcement.

There are lots of other countries who now belong to Interpol today, about 194 or so. The United States pays the largest share of Interpol's yearly budget. According to *Charlie*, it is money well spent, as lots of our crooks move to foreign countries to hide themselves and also to hide their ill-gotten fortunes.

Interpol's Mantra is, "The world only gets smaller for modern day criminals, despots and terrorists, as now days there are no real borders, and close international police cooperation has never been more crucial."

Interpol's Operations include, but are certainly not limited to the following:

A. Locate heinous crooks, fougasses and fugitives, anywhere in the world.

B. Financially, and agent wise, support the great EL Pacto (Europe and Latin America Assistance Program against organized Crime).

C. Issue 'Red Notices' to locate, arrest, and then hold criminals, terrorists and drug kingpins, for extradition.

D. Provide a certified Interpol Incident Response Team that can be fully briefed, equipped and deployed anywhere on the globe, within 12 to 24 hours.

E. Manage 18 police data bases with information on crimes, criminals, war lords, drug cartels, and deplorable terrorists; accessible in real-time to member countries.

F. And many more services, way too many more services that the great Interpol provides, for *Charlie* and his A-Team to list right here.

A few current Interpol's Most Wanted:

1. Admad Omar Saeed Sheikh. He is 43-years old and was born in Tehran, Iran, and now operates out of Canada. He is a known terrorist and has ties to al-Qaeda, in Syria and Iraq, as well as the Taliban, in Afghanistan.

2. Arti Dhir, age 53, born in Nairobi, India and wanted for the murder of a street poor and very innocent 12-year orphan who she adopted, took out a large insurance policy on, and then in 'cold blood' murdered.

3. Harris John Italo Binotti, age 27, born and raised in Myanmar. He killed a fellow teacher at his school, and then fled to nearby Thailand.

4. Omid Tahvili, a native Iranian criminal and terrorist. He is now operating a very large and international criminal enterprise also centered in Canada.

Some of the other most wanted, without the details of their egregious and heinous crimes, and terrorist activities, were:

1. Nour Abdullah G. Ibrahim Hamid.
2.Amin Qatra.
3. Faroulk Hachi.
4. Rouf Uddin.
5.Mohamed Ahmed Hassan.
6. Mohamed Ali Reza.
7. Mohamed Ahmed Youssef.
8. Ahmad Abousomra (Hiding out in Yemen).
9. Gurkan al0Gurhan.
10. Omar al-Sawwaf (Syrian national).

The LAPD and the LASD both wanted these 'bad guys' and wanted them real, real, badly. Police Chief *Michael Moore* and Sheriff *Alex Villanueva*, and the good Mayor of the 'City of the Angels,' *Eric Garcetti*, sat up late many, many nights, to figure out a way to help Charlie and OCSD, LT. Yvette Marie, and the rest of the A-Team, catch these horrible excuses for human beings.

Then in 60 seconds, or less, our man Charles Warner Kennedy 'Charlie' O'Brien, the Private Investigator, was gone...

EPILOGUE

JUST AS LT. YVETTE 'MARIE,' Sarge Hernandez, Lynn and Charles (Charlie) O'Brien, were relaxing on the majestic and crystal clear and deep royal blue Pacific Ocean, by their famous Hotel ('Buena Vista Royale Resort and Spa') in Ensenada, Mexico, Charlie's phone rang to the tune of 'Private Eyes' of course, and Sarge said, "Charlie, my BFF and favorite Jefe, don't answer it, we are on a well-deserved *Symbolical*."

Charlie, just as usual, ignored his mijo and grabbed his satellite cell phone. On the other end of the cell was none other than Donald J. Trump, the POTUS [President of the United States of America].

The President said to Charlie, "Charlie old man, hope you and Sarge and families are staying safe, and staying at home, as much as possible. I know you just finished working on a very heinous and serious bank robbery case in Los Angeles, California, for the great LASD." Then he took a short breath, and then continued, very rapidly.

"And I know you need a well-earned (R and R) rest period, however, I need you and Sarge, with your A-Team to fly to **Buenos Aires**, **Argentina**, South America, immediately, like yesterday."

Charlie responded as fast as he could, "No problem Mr. President, anything for you and the US Government, and we can be on a 'jet plane' at LAX [Los Angeles International Airport--one of the busiest airports in the whole world] in three hours."

The POTUS continued, "The President of Argentina, just called me and told me that they just had just the largest bank robbery in the country's history. The 'Argentina' press and news media are calling it "The Great Buenos Aires Bank Heist."

And, then he closed by saying, "Charlie my old golfing buddy" [Charlie had stayed at Mr. Trump's very lovely and *exquisite* golf club and resort, **Key Lago,** in Florida, and played golf with the President, the excellent Vice President, very strong and intelligent, Mike Pence, and also the great US Attorney General, William 'Bill' Barr], "I knew that I could count on you, you're the best PI in the whole wide world, bar none."

Charlie leaned over to his BFF Sarge, and said, "pack your bag, tell your lovely bride, *Yvette Marie*, bye for now, and that you will *text* her on the plane, we are out of here!"

www.ingramcontent.com/pod-product-compliance
Lightning Source LLC
Chambersburg PA
CBHW030616310726
48979CB00003B/739

* 9 7 8 1 7 3 6 1 4 6 4 1 5 *